Jude's Rescue

Lynn Howard

Jude's Rescue

Lynn Howard © 2023
Published by Twisted Heart Press, LLC

Chapter One

Scottie sat up and muted the show she'd been bingeing the past few hours. She loved the days when there was nowhere to go and nothing to do. She rarely changed from her pajamas on those days.

But something outside, some noise approaching her isolated cabin, had touched her ears and interrupted her coveted 'me time.'

Setting her feet on the ground, she padded in her fluffy socks to the window and peeked through the curtains. Whatever it was, the sound was growing louder.

As the tempest grew closer to her house, she realized the sound was that of dozens of birds of some form, their squawks filling the air and drowning out all other wildlife noises.

It wasn't uncommon for birds to migrate in the cooler months in large groups, but she'd never heard so much damn noise in the time she'd lived in her house.

Scottie grabbed a blanket from the couch and wrapped it around her shoulders then pulled the door open and stepped onto her covered porch. She craned her neck up to look into the sky as dozens upon dozens of birds swarmed overhead.

Except this didn't look like a migration of a flock of birds.

There were hawks *and* crows. The two did not play well together nor did they migrate together.

As she squinted against the setting sun, she watched in awe and shock as the two species dove at each other, pecking with beaks and clawing with talons that looked like large knives.

Periodically, a pair or group of three would fall to the ground, battling each other before one or two would rise into the sky again.

The only explanation was that she currently had a front row seat to a flight Shifter war.

Scottie tended to keep to herself. She stayed under the radar. She rarely, if ever, involved herself in the affairs of Shifters in the area. She'd always been a bit of a loner, had always preferred her solitude to

3

groups. Hence the reason she didn't currently reside within her family Pride's territory. Or with any Pride at all.

Clenching the blanket around her, fingers tight in the fabric, she stared in horror as more and more birds dropped from the sky, never returning to flight. It was a practical massacre, and her front yard was a cemetery.

What the hell was she supposed to do when all these Shifters moved on? Would the friends or family of the fallen come look for their bodies? Or would she end up with a yard full of dead flight Shifters?

From what she could tell, the largest number of dead were crows.

Could these two groups possibly be Black Feather and Skullbone? Just because she didn't insert herself in local Shifter politics didn't mean she wasn't fully aware of what groups inhabited the area, as well as their battles and wars throughout the years.

Yet another reason she kept to herself. She had no desire to fight for a group over something as asinine as territory.

The sounds grew less ear piercing as the numbers of the crows dwindled.

And then a large hawk slammed to the ground not three feet from the last step of her porch.

Scottie slapped a hand over her mouth to hold back a screech. She wasn't afraid, not with the large feline living inside of her, but that had scared the crap out of her. The last thing she'd expected was a bird the size of a large dog to hit the ground with such force only feet from where she stood frozen in shock.

The swarm began to move toward the south as the battle raged on. Those on the ground who could Shift back to their human forms did so and ambled toward where the rest had flown. Those who would never again take another breath remained in her yard, still in their feathered forms.

After surveying the damage done to her yard and wondering how many Shifters would arrive on her property in search of their fallen, she turned her eyes to the giant hawk at the bottom of her steps.

One of its wings looked broken, laying at a weird angle beneath the animal's big body. Its beak was parted, its eyes closed.

But as she took a step closer, she realized the bird still breathed. It wasn't dead.

Jerking her head up, she wondered if there were any other survivors among the fallen.

Running in her socked feet and doing her best to ignore the icky feeling of the cool, wet, muddy ground soaking through her socks, she checked every single bird on the ground, checking for breathing and getting close enough to put her head on their bodies so she could check for a heartbeat.

No. Only the hawk lived. And she had no idea for how long.

But she couldn't let the poor person suffer in the cold while she snuggled under a blanket on her couch.

Scottie crouched down and laid her blanket across the animal. It didn't open its eyes; didn't make a single sound when she grunted and struggled to lift it into her arms and carry it inside. Even with her Shifter strength, this animal was heavy, way heavier and larger than any hawk that existed in the wild.

It was hard to maneuver its wrapped body enough so she could push her door open and carry it inside. After laying it on the couch, she stared down and wondered what the hell she was supposed to do.

What were the birds thinking? They might have been pretty far into the wilderness, but she wasn't the only person who occupied a home this far out. And anyone who paid close enough attention would notice there were far too many birds of different species fighting. They would notice the larger than normal bodies. And, if any others fell the way they had in her yard, humans would end up calling animal control. Or the news. Or both.

Any and all communication with humans over their kind could end up in their extinction. No way would humans simply accept that they shared the planet with men and women who could turn into giant and powerful animals.

The hawk was still wrapped in her blanket on her couch. She'd done her best to avoid jostling its broken wing, but wasn't sure what else she could do for him. Until this Shifter took its skin back, Scottie would have no idea who she was dealing with, whether or not this person would attempt to attack her, whether or not they would have any phone numbers memorized so she could call in some help for him.

All she could do was wait. And patience had never been one of her stronger virtues.

The person on her couch took up more than half the space, so she couldn't get comfortable while she waited.

She should probably put on some real clothes, though. Just in case. She wouldn't change into anything nice or expensive in case she had to Shift on the fly and destroy them, but she wanted to be wearing something more than her PJ bottoms and threadbare shirt when the flight Shifter came to.

With one last glance, she hurried into her room and closed the door softly, quickly changing into a pair of jeans and a long-sleeved tee. She topped her shirt with a long, thick sweater and slid her feet into a pair of house shoe type booties before stepping back out.

There was no longer a hawk lying unconscious on her couch. In its place was a man with shoulder length dark blond hair that was matted near his forehead with blood. He was on his side and his right shoulder looked as though it was dislocated.

All Shifters had the same accelerated healing, but she wasn't sure his bones would slide themselves back into place. She would have to help him set his shoulder back into place or he'd end up healing wrong and could be at a disadvantage if he or his group were attacked again. Even the slightest disabilities among Shifters could bring their death if it hindered their ability to fight.

Scottie froze near her bedroom door. The man's eyes were still closed, he still breathed evenly, but he was massive. She wasn't exactly tiny at five-feet-six-inches, but his body was the entire length of her couch, his feet hanging off the edge near the arm rest.

And he was naked as the day he was born. At least she'd used a blanket to carry him in so his junk and ass were covered. But that left his chest, arms, and lower legs and feet exposed. She didn't tend to keep the heat cranked too high when she was home because she preferred to nest under a pile of blankets when she had the time off.

Tiptoeing back to her bedroom, she grabbed a wet cloth to at least clean the blood from his face and forehead and dragged the comforter from her bed to try to make him a little more comfortable. Once she had him cleaned up and nestled on her couch, she would kick the heat up a few degrees, at least until he woke and told her where he lived so she could contact his Flock.

He stirred a bit as she gently dragged the wet washcloth across his forehead, but his lashes never fluttered, his lids never lifted.

Scottie wasn't exactly a light sleeper, but even she would have woken if someone was rubbing at open wounds.

What if he'd endured some kind of brain damage. She wasn't equipped for something like that. She had very little medical knowledge other than the kind all Shifters knew. Setting bones wasn't exactly outside the norm for her kind since they couldn't go to the hospital for an injury.

She should take the opportunity to set his shoulder while he was out. It could save him the agony of his bones being popped back into place. She knew from experience that having a dislocated joint reset hurt as bad – if not worse – as having it popped out of place.

Tossing the soiled washcloth onto the coffee table, she gripped his arm in her hand and lifted. He was heavy with muscle, his body lean and lithe and bulkier than most flight Shifters she'd met. That definitely explained why his hawk was so massive.

After getting her own body situated and propping a knee on the side of the couch, she twisted and shoved, grunting the same time his joint clicked into place with an audible and loud pop.

Followed by a roar of pain as the man sat straight up, his arms flailing at her and making contact a few times before she dodged out of the way.

Her inner mountain lion hissed and snarled, demanding to be set free to fight off the threat. But this man wasn't a threat. He'd been injured in whatever war he'd been engrossed in above her cabin and property.

She could only hope this guy had been on the right side and hadn't been one of those assholes who felt every female of every species on the planet was there solely for their entertainment.

The man's icy gray eyes finally narrowed on her. He took in the room, looked down his body, then gripped his injured arm, holding it close to his side.

"Who are you?"

"Scottie," she said, ignoring the throb on her arms and torso where his fists had made contact when he'd woken in a panic.

He sat up, but winced, his hand moving from his arm to his side. He then poked and prodded at his head.

"You're hurt. I cleaned up your head the best I could and set your shoulder. But I didn't want to do too much until you were awake."

His brows knitted together as he once more looked around the room as though unable to form a coherent thought. Or maybe he was disoriented.

"Where's my Flock?"

"I don't know," Scottie said. "You fell and I thought you were dead. There are a lot of dead crows in my yard, too. The rest of the birds all flew south. They were still fighting last I saw. You were alive. I couldn't leave you outside. It's supposed to snow tonight. You'd freeze."

His frown deepened. Pushing fully to a sitting position, he swung his legs over the side and tried to stand. Except he swayed and almost went face first into the coffee table.

"Whoa!" Scottie called out, diving for him before he smashed her antique furniture.

Urging him back onto the couch, she kept her eyes averted when she realized he'd dropped both blankets and was currently flashing his twig and berries at the room.

Positioning the bedspread so it would at least cover his lower half, she took a seat on the coffee table across from him.

She supposed she should have been afraid of him. With the amount of muscles covering this man's body added to his height, he looked as though he could snap her in half without breaking a sweat.

But she wasn't some fragile human woman. She had a fierce feline fighter inside of her. Her mountain lion was always up for a good fight.

Which was one of the reasons she worked from home on her laptop and kept her distance from humans as much as possible, only shopping for groceries late at night when most people were tucked away in bed.

"Is there someone I can call for you?" she asked.

A muscle ticked in his jaw and she could see the pain etched in the lines of his face. This close and with him looking her in the eye, she could finally appreciate his rugged beauty. She guessed him to be in his late thirties or perhaps early forties. His jaw was square, and the cutest dimple was centered in the middle of his chin like a damn *Disney* prince.

Why the hell did she have the urge to reach forward and put her fingertip in the center of that adorable dimple that was so at odds with the scowl that appeared permanently etched on his face.

"I don't…" He lifted a hand and pressed it to his forehead. After a slight shake of his head, he dropped his hand. "I don't have my phone. Or clothes," he said, glancing down at himself as though he only then noticed he was butt ass naked on a strange woman's couch.

"Okay. Do you have any numbers memorized? Or can you tell me where your Flock is located? I can either drive you there or let them know you're here. They can bring you clothes and take you home if you don't want to ride with me all…" She waved a hand in his direction. "Naked."

His eyes narrowed and his brows furrowed again.

"You can't remember where your Flock is located?"

"I can't…shit. No. I can't remember where they're located. I can't even remember why I was fighting someone."

"Oh, there were a lot of *someones*. There were dozens of y'all in the air. Which brings me back to the earlier topic – there are a lot of crows in my front yard. They can't stay out there."

"I'm not a crow," he said with a confused frown.

"I know. You were still in your hawk form when I carried you in here."

His eyes jerked to her face. "You carried me in?"

Had she not told him that mere minutes ago? "Yeah. I told you I brought you in because I didn't want you to freeze out there. There's no one else here. I live alone." She caught herself quickly and held up a finger. "Don't get any ideas about forcing a Claim. I have claws and teeth and can cause a lot of damage. Think of me as Sylvester to your Tweety Bird."

The man's lips twitched at the corners and his frown smoothed a touch.

"You can't remember where you live or why you were fighting. How about your name? Let's start there."

He only hesitated a beat before his face lit up with surprise. "Jude. My name is Jude."

"Okay. We're getting somewhere. I assume there aren't a whole lot of hawk Shifters named Jude. Someone has to know about you, know who you're with, know where you belong."

Jude pushed his fingers through his hair, wrinkling his nose when his hand came into contact with the dried, sticky blood. Dropping the hand into his lap, he inhaled deeply and blew it out in a rush.

"What the fuck," he muttered under his breath. "Why can't I remember where the hell I live?"

"You dropped from pretty high up. You hit the ground hard. I thought you were dead. I'd say a little memory loss isn't the worst thing that could have happened."

"I'm in a strange woman's house, naked, with zero memory of my life up until a few minutes ago."

"Hey," she said, laying her hands on his knees in an attempt to comfort him. "You remembered your name. You probably have a mild concussion or something. Give it time. Don't stress or force it. I can wait. In the meantime, did you want to take a shower? I doubt I have any clothes that will fit you, but if you want, I can run out and grab some boxers or sweats or something."

His brows furrowed again, but this time, she couldn't quite decipher the expression.

When he continued to study her face, she squirmed under his scrutiny.

Pulling her hands away, she folded them in her lap. "What?"

"Do we know each other?"

Scottie shook her head. "No. Why?"

"I feel like...we've never met? I feel like I know you."

"Nah. I just have one of those faces. You know, where everyone thinks they recognize me."

Jude shook his head. "No. You have a face I would remember."

The words were a compliment, but he'd said it as a simple statement. Still, she couldn't stop the rush of heat that moved from her chest, up her neck, and settled in her cheeks.

Ducking her head in hope he wouldn't notice, she pushed to her feet and pulled open the linen closet. "Towels are in here. You can use my shampoo or whatever. Sorry if it smells too girly. What size do you wear? I'll get you something to at least cover your...down there," she said, waving her hand toward his crotch.

"You don't have to do that," Jude said.

"Honestly, it's for both of us. It's a little distracting to have a naked, gorgeous man sitting in my house."

The lines on his face smoothed and his eyes widened the slightest bit. "Gorgeous?"

"Oh, please. I'm sure you've looked into a mirror before."

Scottie pulled a towel out of the closet and swung the door shut. She set the towel on the vanity and flipped on the light for him.

"Will you be okay to stand in the shower alone?"

A teasing glint entered Jude's eyes. "If I say no, will you give me a sponge bath?"

The moment the words left his mouth he looked surprised as though he hadn't meant to say the words out loud or like the flirtatious manner was at odds with his personality.

"Make you a deal," she said, leaning against the doorframe. "When you remember your Flock name, I'll personally see to it that you get a sponge bath."

Jude huffed a laugh. "Deal?" He said it more like a confused question than an agreement.

"Back to my question: are you going to be okay if I leave you here? I don't want you to fall and hurt yourself worse. If you think you might pass out or whatever, just wait and I'll help you to the bathroom."

It was Jude's turn to blush. His cheeks took on a bright pink hue as his eyes flitted from her face to his hands that he had folded in front of him.

"You really don't need to buy me anything," he said when she looped her purse over her shoulder and headed toward the front door.

"Trust me – I do. We need to figure out who you really are and where you belong. I can't do that if your schlong is flopping in the wind all day."

His deep, surprised chuckle followed her outside.

Scottie didn't know Jude from the next man, yet she'd felt comfortable enough teasing him about sponge baths and flopping schlongs.

He'd asked if they'd met. Said she'd seemed familiar to him. She knew they'd never met; she knew she would remember a face like his.

But he was right – he felt like he'd been in her life for far longer than less than an hour. There was something about Jude the hawk Shifter that called to her inner lion.

And she was both petrified and exhilarated at the prospect of discovering what that something was.

Jude continued to watch the closed door long after Scottie had stepped through and pulled it shut.

She'd carried him inside. She'd said he'd been embroiled in battle and had fallen to the ground in front of her house.

She'd also said there were dead crow Shifters in her yard.

Pushing to his feet, he waited for the dizziness to fade and parted the curtains to look outside. There were, indeed, several dead crows in her yard.

They would be easy to dispose of, but there was no way Jude would allow Scottie to dig all those holes herself. She would need help.

The problem was he could barely raise his right arm.

Someone would come looking for their people. He knew if someone he cared for died or went missing, he would search for them…

Even if he couldn't remember whether he had someone he cared for or someone who cared for him.

He had to. Scottie had said he was with a large group. That meant he was a member of a large Flock; he'd been fighting alongside them when he'd fallen.

Scottie. What an interesting woman she was. She'd taken him in, tended to his wounds, even set his dislocated shoulder.

And now she was seeking out some clothing for him.

He hated to think of her out there spending money on him, but she was right – they couldn't very well sit around her house while he was naked. His crotch had been hidden behind the thick comforter, but the moment they'd begun to discuss sponge baths, his dick had immediately stood at attention the same time his hawk had perked up and grown curious about the female.

Pushing his fingers through his hair, he grimaced at the sticky blood tangling the shoulder length locks. He'd thought about cutting it for years. Maybe it was time.

For now, though, he needed to clean that crap out of his hair and get the dirt and whatever else coated his skin washed off.

The first few steps toward the bathroom were tentative. He'd managed to stay on his feet without falling over for a few minutes. He should be able to at least stand a few more minutes, long enough for a good shower.

Scottie's cabin was small but cozy. It was a little cool inside. He'd be happy with some real clothing. Although, he was quite enjoying the scent of Scottie being wrapped around him in the form of her comforter.

The bathroom was small. It was fine for a smaller woman, but he stood an inch over six feet and had developed thick muscles over the years of building the homes for his Flock.

Jude turned wide eyes to the mirror. Okay. He did have a Flock. He remembered building the homes. Things were clicking into place, though they were slow to come and only bits and pieces. But it was a start.

The pipes squeaked as he turned the spigot and started the shower. He waited until steam rose in the air before stepping in and pulling the curtain closed behind him.

For the first half of his shower, he simply stood under the spray and let the hot water rinse the blood and dirt from his hair and body. He figured there had to be a decent gash on his scalp to have caused so much blood. His animal would help heal it, but for now, he had no desire to scrub at an open wound any more than necessary.

Scottie had warned him about the toiletries he'd have to use, but he wasn't quite prepared for how sweet and citrusy they would all smell. He would smell like a chick by the time he was done. But at least he would be clean.

His hair was the last thing he washed. When he couldn't put it off any further, he poured a little of Scottie's shampoo into his hand and lathered up his hair as best he could with minimal use of one arm. It wasn't nearly as painful as he'd feared, but there was definitely a sting when the soap hit the open wound. Quickly rinsing it off, he grit his teeth as the water rinsed the soap and blood away.

Ending the spray, Jude pulled the curtain open and reached for a towel hanging on the rack. As he rubbed it down his face to dry the droplets, he couldn't help but inhale Scottie's scent deep into his lungs.

Honestly, he had no idea why the hell he'd done that. He didn't know the female. She'd confirmed they'd never met, but that didn't stop the sense of familiarity. More than familiarity – she felt as though she was important to his life. Or perhaps she was meant to become important to his life.

Fuck. Not knowing who he was, why he was there, or whether there was anyone in his life looking for him was screwing with his head.

The towel was soft and fluffy against his skin. At least there was that. Small and inconsequential, but still somewhat of a win.

Once he was dry, he wrapped the towel around his waist, gathered the blanket he'd had wrapped around himself when he'd woken, and carried it into the living room.

Scottie was unloading bags onto the coffee table. She glanced at him over her shoulder, back to her purchases, then did a quick double take, her eyes going wide as they scanned his body from head to toe.

"Holy crap," she whispered.

Both embarrassment and a surge of manly pride washed over him. He had the urge to lift his arms and cross them over his chest even though he had nothing to hide up there.

"Sorry. I didn't know you were back," he said.

14

Would he have wrapped himself in the blanket if he'd heard her come in? Being half naked didn't feel like something he should have been embarrassed about. He might not have remembered shit, but being naked – or half naked – felt completely natural to him.

"It's fine," she said, waving her hand in the air as she quickly turned back to the pile of fabric and other goods laid out on the table. "I got you some clothes and toiletries. I didn't think you'd want to keep using my stuff while we figure out where you belong."

She kept her back to him as she held out a stack of what appeared to be sweatpants.

Taking the clothing from her hand, he pulled the dark gray pants up his legs and under the towel. "I'm covered," he announced, unable to suppress the grin that stretched across his face.

She turned and handed him a shirt.

"You're still way too distracting like that," she said, keeping her eyes averted.

"Aren't you a Shifter?" he asked as he tugged the tee over his head.

He'd caught the faint smell of fur in her house and any time she was close. Unless she hung around Shifters, there was no way she would smell of fur and be so calm after watching him turn from a hawk into a man. In fact, the moment she'd spotted so many birds fighting in her yard and then had one crash to the ground outside of her house, she would have called animal control.

"Yeah. Why?"

"Then why does my bare chest distract you?"

Her brows shot up her forehead and her eyes widened. "Seriously? Have you looked in a mirror?"

That surge of manly pride washed over him again when he caught the slightest hint of her arousal.

Unfortunately, the pants she'd purchased for him did little to hide his boner.

Cupping his hands in front of him and aiming for casual, he pretended to check out the other items Scottie had purchased.

She eyed him a second, then held up some shampoo. "You already showered, but I got you some manly smelling stuff. Shampoo, bodywash, deodorant, and a toothbrush. I wasn't sure what else you would need. I'm hoping we can find your people soon."

"I can go somewhere else if I'm imposing," Jude said. He hadn't considered the fact he might have been interrupting her life. If she had a mate or was dating someone, his presence could cause a lot of friction.

But he didn't smell the change that happened in a woman's blood when she was marked by her true mate. So, if she happened to have a man in her life, he wasn't the one she was meant to spend her life with…meaning Jude still had a chance.

He blinked a few times as the thoughts ran through his head. What the hell was going on with his brain? Maybe he'd done more damage than he'd realized.

"You're not imposing. I work from home, but I took the day off. You're fine."

He took the bag of socks from her hand and pulled a pair free. After slipping them over his feet, he stood again and looked through the window.

"I need to get those crows away from your house." He focused hard and then turned back to her. "You didn't see any other hawks fall?"

She shook her head. "Just you."

Sucked that he'd been bested, but at least there were no others of his kind littering her yard.

"Should we bury them?" Scottie asked.

"I don't know. I'm sure their people will eventually come looking for them. I don't want anyone showing up here thinking you killed members of their group."

"I highly doubt someone's going to think my mountain lion attacked a group of crows midflight. Besides, I saw the battle. There were a lot of birds going crazy out there. No way would they think those people died from anything but the fight."

He nodded, lifting his hand to scratch at the stubble peppering his cheeks and chin. "Any chance you bought a razor?"

"No. But you can use mine. I don't have any shaving cream, though."

"It's cool. Like you said, hopefully I won't be here long."

16

As he said the words, an odd twinge of pain stabbed him in the center of his chest. His heart felt like it had slivered a little at the realization he would eventually walk away from Scottie and possibly never see her again.

Chapter Two

Now that Jude's unbelievable body was covered, Scottie was able to focus on more important matters, like figuring out where the hell he lived and which Flock he belonged to.

The only two she knew of were Black Feather and Skullbone, but she knew there were more in the state than that. Was there a chance this battle had moved far from home, or were they simply two local groups vying over territory or women as so many other groups had?

"I know I wasn't gone long, but anything else come to you in that time?"

His broad shoulders rose and fell. "Not much. I remember building homes for members of my Flock. And that I was a member of a Flock."

His shoulders shrugged up again, but this time, a little sadness entered his eyes.

"Hey. Don't freak out. We'll figure it out. Someone will be looking for you. There were a lot of hawks up there. I'm sure once your people regroup, they'll notice you missing. They'll eventually backtrack."

She reached up and touched her fingers to his cheek, his stubble prickling her skin.

Jude nuzzled her hand, and she couldn't force herself to pull away. It felt so natural, his face in her hand, his body so close to hers.

His eyes darted to her lips and then he took a quick step away like he'd snapped out of some stupor.

She knew the feeling. For a moment there, she'd felt as if she were drowning in the iciness of his gray eyes.

Dropping her hand to her side, she shoved both in her pockets and rocked back on her heels. "You've got to be starving after all that."

"Yeah," he said, his voice deeper and a little husky.

Ohhh. They needed to keep themselves under control or her inner cat was going to get a little feisty. She was pretty sure felines and birds weren't the best match. At least not in the wild.

But they weren't in the wild, were they?

18

Shaking the thoughts from her overactive imagination, she turned and hurried to the kitchen, rummaging through her fridge and cabinets until she found something she could throw together quickly.

"Pasta okay?" she asked as she pulled out some noodles and sauce.

"Fine," he said.

And, yeah, his voice was still deep and husky.

The springs squeaked as Jude lowered onto the couch. "I don't have any garlic bread or salad or anything cool for a side," Scottie said.

"It's fine. Pasta works," he said.

While she waited for the water to boil, she dug out two beers from the fridge.

"I know it's early, but do you want a beer?"

"It's not that early," he said, looking toward the window.

The sun was beginning to set, but it was creeping in on winter and sun was setting earlier every day. It was barely five o'clock.

Although…neither of them had anywhere they needed to be anytime soon. Not until they figured out where the hell he belonged.

A stab to her heart made her jump. Pressing her hand over her chest, she rubbed the heel over the spot. What the hell had that been? As soon as she'd entertained the thought of Jude leaving her home and disappearing forever, a strange pain had immediately taken root in her heart.

Handing Jude a beer, she turned her back on him and pretended to check the status of the water and noodles. She really didn't want him to see the hurt and disappointment in her eyes over something she had no business or right to be affected by.

"Just a few more minutes," she said.

Taking a long pull from the beer, she set it on the counter and retrieved plates from the cabinets, setting them on her small two-seater table in the corner of the kitchen.

Her home had never felt small to her, but she'd never had someone Jude's size hanging out there…or anyone at all, for that matter. She never had company, not even her family or anyone from her family Pride.

Jude's face twisted in pain as he slowly pushed to his feet and slowly ambled to the table.

"I'm sorry. I could have brought it to you."

He shook his head. "I'll be fine. I'll heal."

"But you're in pain. It sucks. Let me take care of you until you're one hundred percent."

One of Jude's blond brows raised and a sexy smirk quirked up one side of his mouth.

"Okay, perv. I meant your wounds."

He barked out a surprised laugh, then clamped his lips together.

Scottie's cheeks burned, but she couldn't hold back her chuckle. They might not have known each other before this morning, but he was right – he felt so familiar to her. It felt more as though they'd been friends for years.

"I'm going to go try to figure out what to do with the dead crows. I can't leave them out there like that, even if they were your enemy," she said.

"Wait," he called after her. "I'll help."

Glancing down at his sock clad feet, she raised her attention to his face. "You're wearing socks. And you were out cold less than two hours ago. Rest. I've got it."

As she pulled the door closed, it was pulled out of her hand.

Scottie raised both brows and stared up into his face.

"Seriously?"

"I might not remember shit about my life prior to a couple hours ago, but I'm pretty sure it goes against everything I stand for to allow a woman to go out to deal with the enemy alone."

"I'm not exactly dealing with anyone," she said, watching as he bent and pulled off first one sock then the other. "I'm disposing of…well, dead people. Dead birds. Dead…crow Shifters. Okay, yeah. That whole line of wording felt weird to say out loud."

His deep chuckle warmed her and made her heart do a funny little flip in her chest.

"You're going to go barefoot in the yard when it's barely above freezing."

His broad shoulders shrugged up. "I've been naked in this weather. What's the difference?"

Yes. He had been naked in this weather. And she'd had a front row seat for it. The image was pretty much seared in her mind, regardless of how hard she'd tried not to notice his lower half when she'd covered him on the couch.

He moved past her, his strides steady, his long legs eating up space. She nearly jogged to catch up to him.

Jude lowered and began to lift dead crows, piling them in his arms. When there were too many, he would start a pile then go for more.

"What are we going to do with them? It feels wrong to throw them away. Burn them? Bury them? Not like you know who these people would belong to."

He tilted his head and studied the pile. "Black Feather," he blurted. Then he turned quickly and stared at her with wide eyes. "They're part of Black Feather. Holy shit." He breathed the last part.

"Awesome! Your memory is coming back," she said. "I don't suppose you know who I can contact about them?"

The grunt that he emitted was, to her ears, part sarcastic, part amused, and part frustrated.

"Okay. I've heard of them. I've also heard of a group called Skullbone Flock. Does that one sound familiar?"

His eyes narrowed and averted as though thinking.

"Don't stress. I'll go to that bar…uh…Moe's, I think. I'll ask around to see if I can contact someone from Black Feather."

She turned to him and let her eyes roam his body.

"Actually, maybe I should contact Skullbone first, see if you're one of their missing people. If I find Black Feather and they find you here…"

"Good idea," he said.

He turned on his heel and headed back to the house. Jude looked beside him, then stopped and turned to look at her. "We going?"

Scottie jogged to catch up again. "You're going with me? Without shoes?"

"Again. We're Shifters, Scottie."

"We might get naked when we Shift, but that doesn't mean we run around in public like a bunch of Neanderthals."

21

There was that deep chuckle again. She so loved that sound, loved the way it made her feel all warm and fuzzy yet gushy at the same time.

He stopped near the driveway. "Shit. I flew here." He turned and rubbed the back of his neck.

"Looks like you're going to have to fold your big ass into my car," she teased. "Let me grab my purse and keys."

Hurrying inside, she grabbed her stuff, locked the door, and hurried out to where Jude waited by her car, his thick arms crossed over his chest.

She should have bought him a jacket or at least a hoodie. It was way too chilly for his arms to be exposed. No matter how many times he talked about the natural state of Shifters when they let their animals take their forms, they weren't currently Shifted. The wind and cool air would still sting against bare flesh.

Hitting the button on her fob, she unlocked the doors and then hit the AutoStart button, hoping to get the car warmed up for Jude faster. She wasn't exactly bundled up in a coat and gloves, but she had more coverage than he did.

"Sorry. My car takes a minute to heat up," she said as she pulled the car out of her spot and down her driveway.

"It's fine," he said.

But his muscles were tense, and she could only assume it was either from the cold or the tension of not knowing where he belonged. Oh, and the pile of dead crows they'd left behind in her yard.

The moment warm air began to blow from the vents, she reached down and turned up the blower, aiming the heat toward Jude the best she could.

"I'm really okay," he said. "I tend to run warm."

"Yeah, but it's not even forty degrees today. Hot blooded or not, it's chilly outside."

And they'd spent some time outdoors gathering the fallen birds.

It was odd to have someone of Jude's size in her passenger seat, his long legs cramped up in front of the dash. Unfortunately, the seat didn't go back any further, so it was the best she could offer.

She had a feeling he drove a monster sized truck, one of those lifted kinds that would take a step ladder for her to climb into. Whatever he drove, it would have to fit his big body.

Smooshed in her car or not, she loved the way his natural scent mixed with her products he'd used in the shower. She loved the way his scent completely filled the cab of her car, the way it seemed to soak into her pores.

Coming just short of inhaling as deeply as she could and making a complete fool of herself, Scottie turned the radio up a tad. "Are you warmed up?"

"Yeah. Thank you," he said, shooting her a sheepish smile.

"I knew it. You were freezing and trying to act all tough."

The sheepish smile stayed in place and a soft pink colored his whisker covered cheeks. He didn't have a full beard, but rather looked as though he hadn't bothered to shave in a few days out of either a busy life or laziness.

She didn't care what his reasons were for not shaving; the whiskers gave him an air of rugged sexiness. Whether or not they ever saw each other again, she was a female and he was male. She was allowed to appreciate an example of perfect masculinity.

Jude should have been excited about the prospect of putting the missing pieces of his life into place. But the further they drove from Scottie's, the higher his anxiety grew.

The unknowns. All the unknowns were what caused his heart to race and his palms to sweat.

Wiping his hands back and forth along the soft cotton of his sweats, he inhaled deeply through his nose and blew it out slowly through his mouth.

"You okay?" Scottie asked.

She glanced at him as she rolled the car to a stop at a light.

"Yeah," he lied.

No. He wasn't okay. He was a wreck. Fear riddled his thoughts, but he couldn't figure out what the hell he was afraid of. He was a big dude. He'd apparently been in battle when he'd fallen from the sky onto Scottie's yard. As he thought about facing a possible enemy, he realized it wasn't fear for himself, but fear for Scottie. He didn't want her condemned simply by her association to Jude.

"This is a bad idea," he blurted.

Scottie pulled one hand from the wheel and laid it on his, squeezing it while it rested on his thigh.

"It'll be fine. We'll see if anyone recognizes you, maybe ask a few questions. If we don't get any answers today, we'll try again tomorrow. I'll be there with you the whole time."

She squeezed once more and went to pull away.

But Jude tightened his hold, keeping her hand right where it was.

"I'm not worried about me," he admitted.

"Then what are you worried about?"

He turned and looked at her profile as she flipped on the blinker and turned onto the gravel lot of Moe's Tavern.

"What if someone thinks you're with me. If one of the people I was fighting is in there, they might come after you to get to me."

She scoffed. Once the car was in park, she turned her upper body to look into his face. "I'm not some damsel in distress, Jude. I can take care of myself. I've lived alone for the past ten years. And don't think I haven't had to deal with my share of assholes. My cat likes to fight. A lot. I'll be completely fine."

She smiled, the simple look sending arrows straight to his heart.

"But thank you for worrying about me."

She lifted his hand and pressed her lips to the back of his knuckles before releasing her hold and pushing the door open.

Jude looked down at his hand. It tingled where her lips had touched. Odd.

With less gusto than Scottie, he opened the car door and stepped out of his side. She waited at the hood of the car, her brows raised and a soft smile on her full lips.

He really should have been ecstatic over the possibility of finding his people and putting his life back together. But that meant walking away from Scottie. He'd only spent a few hours with her, yet he wanted more. He wanted to get to know her, find out what she did that she was able to work from home, find out why she didn't live with a Pride.

Find out why she wasn't yet mated.

She appeared to be somewhere near her early thirties. It wasn't rare for females to find their mates a little later in life, but it wasn't exactly common.

Scottie made it to the door before Jude. Lunging forward, he gripped the handle and yanked the door open, stepping in directly behind her to protect her back while keeping an eye on anyone ahead of her.

The sounds of pool balls clicking together mixed with the soft hum of the radio and raised conversation. Stale cigarette smoke and the smell of old beer tickled his nose.

All of it felt familiar, yet he couldn't remember when or if he'd actually been to Moe's. If it was a Shifter bar, he could only assume he had.

"Holy shit," someone said above the throng of noise.

A male with dark hair pushed to his feet so quickly his chair almost toppled, and he hurried to where Scottie and Jude stood.

Jude instantly stepped ahead of Scottie, using his body to shield her.

"We thought you were dead. We looked everywhere. Where the fuck were you?" the dark-haired man asked, pulling Jude into a back slapping hug.

A light hand touched his back and Jude knew it was Scottie offering him strength and comfort. He knew her touch already after such a short period of time with her.

The man pulled back and Jude was astonished to see a glimmer in his gray eyes.

"Jude?" the man asked.

A few others stood and made their way to where they stood, their eyes wide, looks of relief and astonishment evident on their faces.

"Um," Scottie said, moving forward until she stood beside Jude. Her arm brushed his, her warmth comforting him in an odd way. "He doesn't remember you. He was hurt after you…wait, how do I know you're his friend and not trying to trick him?"

The dark-haired man looked at Scottie and frowned.

"What? Trick him how?"

These people had no idea that Jude had lost his memory. There was no way they could use it against him.

"Scottie found me after…whatever happened. The battle."

"He was hurt pretty badly. He must have gotten a pretty bad head injury because he can't remember anything more than his name. And that he'd helped build houses for his people." She thrust her hand forward. "I'm Scottie. Are you…are you guys with Skullbone?"

"Yeah," the dark-haired man said, his face a mask of confusion and concern.

Jude and Scottie were guided to a table with several males with gray eyes. They were all hawks like Jude. The faces felt familiar, but Scottie's had, too. And she'd confirmed they'd never met before this afternoon.

"Dude, are you alright?" another man asked.

This shit sucked ass. He felt like an idiot staring at these people who obviously knew and cared for him and he couldn't remember their names or a single conversation before tonight.

"Yeah. Yeah, I'm alright," he said.

He pushed his fingers through his hair and looked to Scottie. He barely knew her, but she felt safe. She felt like a lifeline.

"Why don't we sit down and see if we can't figure this all out." Scottie grabbed his hand and linked her fingers through his.

He'd been so concerned about her safety, yet she was the one being strong for him.

Squeezing her fingers lightly, he followed the dark-haired male to a table full of people.

"What the fuck happened?" The dark-haired guy frowned. "I'm Luca, by the way," he said after they were all seated.

"I don't know," Jude admitted. "Scottie said there was a battle."

"Yeah. The Black Feather Crew attacked us midflight. It turned into a big ol' brawl –"

"That flew right over my cabin," Scottie interjected.

"Sorry about that," Luca said with a tip of his head.

"There are some dead crows in my yard. We were hoping…" She turned and looked into Jude's face before turning back to Luca. "We're not sure what to do with them. I don't want your enemy showing up at my house and accusing me of being a part of any of it."

"I'll send out some people to clear the bodies."

"Shouldn't you contact Black Feather? Wouldn't they want to bury their dead?" Scottie asked.

Jude raised a brow at Luca. But he was looking at Jude as though waiting for the answer.

"Dude," a man said. "You're the Alpha. We need the answer from you."

"Oh shit," Scottie breathed from beside him.

"I…" Jude had no idea what to say. He had no idea what the right answer was.

On one hand, if someone he cared for was killed, he would want them to have a proper goodbye and burial. But on the other, the last thing he wanted was for a group of people who apparently hated Jude and his people – it was weird as hell to think he led this group – to show up at Scottie's while she was alone.

Or at all. He would prefer any asshole who would attack a group while they were midflight to be nowhere near Scottie or her home.

Scottie pulled their clasped hands onto her thigh and held it tightly.

Looking into her honey-colored eyes, he searched for the answer, searched for a glimmer of who he was before he'd woken on her couch.

Luca leaned forward, resting his elbows on the table. "Why don't we head back to the territory, get you some clean clothes, and figure it out there."

"Hey, those are clean. I just bought them. He didn't go, so he couldn't try them on," Scottie said.

Jude smiled over at her faux pout.

She winked at him. "It sounds like a good idea. At least then you'll know where you live."

There was an obvious tease in her tone. But he was mildly nervous about returning to a place full of strangers. He knew somewhere deep inside the males at this table were important to him, but he still didn't recognize them. They felt familiar, but so had Scottie.

"We'll follow you back to the territory," Scottie said.

"We can take him home. Thank you for your help," Luca said.

"Oh. Okay." Scottie turned an unsure and sad smile on Jude. "You know where to find me if you ever need another crash pad."

She scooted her chair and moved to stand, but Jude tightened his hold on her hand and kept her in her seat.

"I'll ride with Scottie," he said.

If he really was the Alpha, he assumed the males would acquiesce to his wishes. And that involved riding with Scottie to the place where he supposedly lived, to the people he supposedly led.

Shouldn't it make him feel weak that he needed this woman to join him when being reunited with his Flock?

Nah. He might not have remembered much about his life prior to Scottie's living room, but he knew deep inside he loved strong women.

Chapter Three

The tension and suspicion were palpable. And Scottie didn't blame Jude's people one bit. All they knew was that some stranger showed up with their Alpha, who had no memories of his life before the battle. If Scottie were in their shoes, she would probably think she had ulterior motives, as well.

They all filed out to their vehicles, Jude's hand still entwined with hers. She wanted to believe it was because he simply wanted to touch her but knew she was an anchor for him, one solid thing in the middle of all this craziness.

Scottie couldn't imagine how confusing and scary it would be to lose her memories. Although there were more than a few she would be happy to lose.

But as a whole, not remembering who she was or where she belonged would be terrifying.

At least his people seemed understanding and patient. They'd let him know he was their Alpha and had deferred to him when it came to making a decision about the dead Shifters in her yard.

He opened her car door and waited for her to lower into her seat before heading to his side. It was date-like behavior, but she hadn't missed the way his eyes scanned the parking lot vigilantly as he'd rounded the hood.

"Your friends seem nice," she said as he pulled his belt into place.

He grunted. "I thought…" He shook his head.

"You thought your memory would come back if you saw your people?"

"Yeah."

He sounded so sad. If they weren't in her car and filing behind a line of vehicles, she might have climbed onto his lap so she could hug him. She wasn't the kind of female to trust easily, but like Jude had said earlier, they felt like old friends. He felt familiar to her. They might not have known each other before the battle, but her heart recognized him as someone extremely important to her life.

And her cat had purred in her head nonstop since he'd pulled her back to her chair inside Moe's and kept his hand wrapped around hers.

"It'll be okay. I know it's weird right now, but they all seem like they really care for you."

It was her turn to feel sad. But she pushed it aside. This wasn't about her. This was about helping Jude get his life back on track. He was the Alpha of Skullbone Flock. That was a pretty damn big deal.

Every single one of those males at the table had seemed genuinely relieved to see their leader walk through the door. Many of them had had tears glimmering in their eyes as they'd watched with nothing short of awe on their faces when they realized their leader hadn't been killed.

The trip to Skullbone Flock territory didn't take long. Fifteen minutes after pulling from the bar's lot, the first truck turned onto a bumpy, dirt road that went on for close to a quarter mile before small homes came into view.

They weren't quite cabins, but they weren't fully houses, either. She would be surprised if more than one of the hawk Shifters could fit inside them at a time. They weren't as tall or broad as the bartender back at Moe's, but they were all six-feet and over. The door leading into the first house looked like it would skim the top of their heads when they passed through.

"This is nice," she said, leaning forward and squinting at the houses illuminated by the several pairs of headlights.

"I remember building them," he said softly. "I smacked my thumb with a hammer when we were working on that one," he said, pointing to the third house. "And that one is mine."

Pointing at the first house, he quickly turned and raised his brows at Scottie.

"That's awesome! It's coming back!"

A smile stretched across his face, showcasing straight, white teeth. All the sadness drained from his face when he smiled like that. And something warmed her heart when he smiled at her like that.

She loved to see people happy. Not that she had much opportunity to see happiness on anyone's faces with her self-imposed isolation.

When Jude pushed from the car, he seemed much lighter, his head turning this way and that as he surveyed his territory.

"Fuck. Okay. I remember the houses. Why can't I remember the people?" he muttered to her as she joined him at the hood.

"Give it time. This is a huge step," she said, raising a hand and rubbing slow circles on his back in what she hoped was a reassuring gesture.

Luca and the other males waited for him to join them. Instead of moving toward one of the houses, they led the way to a covered but open area with a large fire pit positioned in the center of a circle of chairs.

"You know I'm Luca. I'm your Second," Luca said.

"Burke," a man with strawberry blond hair said with a raised hand.

Two others introduced themselves until all five men had announced their names.

"Anything?" Luca asked.

"You all feel familiar. I just…no," Jude said.

Luca looked to the redhead. Burke nodded and stood, stepping into one of the cabins and emerging with a cooler.

Setting it at his feet, he opened the lid and began to pass out bottles of beer.

"It's cool. You remember the houses. That's something," Burke said.

Scottie looked to each person as they spoke. They entered an easy conversation like they were trying to put Jude at ease and make him feel like it was simply a normal day. And who knew? The normalcy might help jog his memory.

Jude's body language was tense, but he laughed when something was funny and periodically brushed his fingertips across Scottie's hand that sat on the armrest.

It felt good that he depended on her for comfort. Maybe that sounded selfish, but it had been so damn long since she'd made a true connection with another person, since she'd let someone in, that she was warmed by his need for her comfort.

The sun had set a while ago and the air had gone from cool to downright chilly. Because she hadn't planned on spending much time outside, she hadn't bothered to bring a coat or gloves or anything to bundle up at all.

A shiver shook her body, and she instinctively crossed her arms over herself, tucking her hands into her armpits to warm them up.

"Someone light a fire," Jude said after a quick glance at Scottie.

"No. It's okay. I should probably get going soon anyway. I'm sure you guys have a lot to talk about. Like who's going to come get the dead crows out of my yard."

She tried to keep her tone light, but she really, *really* wanted someone to remove the Shifters sooner rather than later. It was a little morbid that there were at least a dozen dead Shifters stacked in a pile on her property.

"She's right. We need to get that taken care of before Black Feather comes looking for their fallen members," Jude said.

"*Will* they come looking? They're not exactly known for their loyalty," Luca said.

"I don't want to take the chance. She lives in complete isolation. It's too much of a risk," Jude said.

When he turned his eyes toward her, she could have sworn she'd seen a hint of silver glow in his irises. Anger. Anger over the thought of his enemy trespassing on her property. That had to be it.

Right?

She didn't blame him. She barely knew Jude and his people and hated the thought of anyone who wished them harm coming anywhere near them. Especially Jude.

"What will we do with the bodies?" Burke asked.

"I really think you should at least talk to Black Feather's Alpha, see if he wants to collect his fallen members," Scottie suggested.

The way everyone looked at her made her feel as though she'd grown a third eye or second head.

"All I'm saying is it might cause more problems if you simply dispose of his people like they were roadkill. Think of how you would feel if any of those people who'd fallen had been hawks."

"One of them *was* a hawk," Luca said.

"Yeah, but he lived. The crows didn't. Whether you guys have some lifelong beef against each other or not, I'm sure the Alpha would want to at least know the number of his losses. And maybe collect them for a proper burial, let their families tell them goodbye."

Jude looked to Luca. She had no idea whether that was normal in their Flock but couldn't imagine the Alpha of her family Pride consulting with any of the other mountain lions, even his Second. He saw it as beneath him. His word was law and all that crap.

"We'll make a call and go as a group. Call a couple of the bears and wolves, see if they'd be willing to join in case backup is needed," Jude said.

He might not have remembered that he was the Alpha, but he was a natural in the role. He was a natural leader.

Luca stood and pulled his phone from his pocket, pacing away as he made a call. His voice rose a few times, but he kept his temper in check.

When he ended the call, he returned to the circle, rubbing his forehead as though a headache formed behind his eyes. She was sure the call went about as well as she imagined. What Alpha wanted to be contacted by their rival and alerted to a pile of dead bodies?

Once Luca was seated, he tapped on his screen several times, presumably sending a text to the friends Jude had mentioned.

Wait...

"You remembered you were friends with bears and wolves!" Scottie said, turning a grin on Jude. "You mentioned calling them in for backup. You're almost there!"

His smile grew until it matched hers. And then he surprised her by leaning forward and pressing his lips to hers in a quick kiss.

It wasn't romantic or heated. It was a kiss of gratitude and excitement.

Her brain was fully aware of that, but the knowledge did nothing to quell the heat that pooled low in her belly.

Why the hell was he getting so stressed about his memory loss? It hadn't been a full day yet. And already, things were beginning to fall into place.

Several of their friends agreed to meet Skullbone at Scottie's house. He hated to give out her address, hated that so many people would know where she lived, but his friends were good, honorable people who'd done nothing but protect females of all species for as long as he'd known them.

Now, Jude sat in the passenger seat of Scottie's car again. He supposed he could have ridden with one of his friends or taken his own vehicle. Any of the trucks behind them would have had plenty of room for his long legs.

But he wanted to spend more time with Scottie. There was a chance their fast friendship could end after tonight. Though he would prefer they get closer rather than drift apart. If it were up to him, he would stay the night in her bed. Not necessarily naked – not that he would mind – but simply holding her.

In the short time they'd spent together, she'd come to mean so much to him. Her simple touches, the way she took his hand or rubbed circles on his back when she sensed his anxiety – they all felt like gestures and actions by a couple who'd learned all there was to know about each other.

His hawk stretched its wings in his head and perked up, paying close attention to the situation.

Minutes later, Scottie pulled her car onto her driveway and circled around to the front, leaving plenty of room for the others to pull in behind her.

She gave Jude a soft smile before stepping out of her side. He was as reluctant to climb from his seat as he'd been at the bar.

This time, though, was because he didn't want to leave at the end of this ordeal. He wanted to spend more time with Scottie. He wanted to get to know everything he could about her, to feel her lips against his again. Only this time, he planned to take his time exploring her mouth instead of the quick, joy filled press of lips he'd given her around the fire pit.

While she hadn't done anything that was outwardly flirtatious – short of offering a sponge bath – he'd scented her arousal more than once in their day together. He could only hope she was feeling the same pull he was.

After procrastinating too long, he pushed the door open and unfolded himself from the seat. His people were surveying the pile of crows, wearing matching expressions ranging from disgust to anger.

Gravel crunched under tires, heralding the arrival of more vehicles. Jude caught the scent of fur before he turned. Their friends had arrived.

As men filed from trucks and SUVs, he recognized faces yet still couldn't place names with each person. At least he was getting somewhere. His brain was slowly yet surely putting all the pieces into place.

And Scottie had been such a big part of helping him get this far. She'd been so patient, had bought him clothing so he wouldn't sit around naked, had taken him to the one place a number of Shifters would congregate in hopes of finding his people.

"Hey, man! Good to see you're alright," a man who stood a few inches taller than Jude said as he approached with an outstretched hand.

The face was familiar, Jude knew they were friends, but he still couldn't remember any names.

Gripping the man's hand, he was mildly surprised when the lumbering man pulled Jude into a rough hug complete with hard back slaps.

"He doesn't know who you are," Luca said.

The man pulled away, his hands still on Jude's shoulders, and frowned at him.

"You know me, man," the male said, his voice carrying a hint of a southern accent.

"He had a head injury during the battle," Scottie explained. "He's having some trouble remembering anything before this morning."

"I know your face," Jude said with a shrug.

"Colton. I'm Colton with Blackwater."

Jude looked to the other males and gave a nod of appreciation, grateful when no one looked on him with pity. His memory was slowly returning so it was just a matter of time before it all came back to him.

Including the names of the males standing around watching him as they waited for the Alpha of Black Feather Crew to arrive.

"How do you think this will go down?" a male asked. When Jude frowned at him, he tipped his head. "Gray. Alpha of Big River Pack."

"Sorry, man," Jude said.

"Nah. No need. We get it. We're just happy you're okay," Gray said, gripping Jude's shoulder and giving it a squeeze.

Frustration built in his chest. He really needed to be more patient, more understanding that his animal was doing its best to heal a near fatal injury.

They stood around talking and catching up while they waited for members of Black Feather to arrive.

A vehicle slowed in the driveway with a squeal of bad brakes the same time crows squawked overhead. They were coming in both forms.

Everyone tensed. Males split their attention between watching the headlights bump up the driveway and the dark sky.

"You should wait inside," Jude said to Scottie, pushing her behind him with a hand on her hip.

"Oh, please. I already told you – my cat would love to chase after some asshole birds."

Several male chuckles sounded around the field, breaking through the tension.

"Want me to Shift? I'd love to see the look on their faces when they find a big cat waiting for them."

Jude turned and smiled down at Scottie. He didn't think she was being serious, but she'd successfully eased the tension in his shoulders and back.

"They've seen giant cat Shifters. But I would still feel better if you waited inside. You're the only female out here."

"So?"

"He's trying to tell you he's worried he'll attack unprovoked if one of the crows pay too much attention to you," Luca said.

Well shit. That actually hadn't been his first thought, but now that Luca had mentioned it...

"Fine. I'll wait inside. Holler if you need me," Scottie said, running her hand down Jude's arm before jogging into the cabin.

The moment the door closed behind her, he realized why she felt so familiar, why her presence was so comforting, why he worried about her safety above all others.

Mine…

His hawk declared Scottie as his mate.

So fucked up that his animal chose its natural predator for its soul mate.

Two vehicles pulled behind the row of trucks, leaving enough space for them to turn with ease if they needed to haul ass away from Skullbone and their friends. Crows began to land in the field, leaving plenty of distance to Shift to their skin if the males ended up going fisticuffs.

Jude crossed his arms over his chest and glared as a male approached, flanked by four others. Their faces were completely unfamiliar, and Jude feared they would learn he'd lost his memory.

"You killed my men," the male said.

"Your people attacked us," Luca said.

That much of the story Jude had already learned. He'd found out his Flock had been attacked in mid-flight and the battle had somehow moved until they were directly over Scottie's place.

"Where are they?" the male in charge asked.

Jude had no idea who this male was but wouldn't ask his name, not in front of him, anyway. It would be a sign of weakness. No fucking way would he show an ounce of weakness in front of his enemy.

Jerking his head, he motioned toward the pile of crows.

"What the fuck?!" the leader bellowed as he stomped to where Scottie and Jude had left the bodies. "You left them out here like a pile of trash."

"Shame we didn't toss them in a dumpster," Luca replied, making sure the Black Feather leader heard him.

Crows began to land, hopping to where their fallen friends laid in a pile. One by one, they Shifted to their human forms and began to gather the crows in their arms.

Glares were shot in the direction of the Skullbone Flock as well as their friends as they passed.

The dead crows were deposited into the waiting vehicles. The naked males Shifted back and took flight, landing on limbs high above everyone's heads.

"They're not sticking around here," Jude said.

Shit. He needed to keep his mouth shut. He didn't want any of those fuckers to know Scottie meant anything to him or they could and *would* use her to get to him. She might have been able to fight, her animal might have been scrappy, but that didn't mean she could take on several Shifter males at once.

"My Crew will do what the fuck they want, asshole."

A very human and very angry growl rumbled up from his chest and escaped through his parted lips. He knew without asking that his eyes would be blazing a bright silver and his skin prickled with the need to Shift.

A firm hand wrapped around Jude's bicep and tugged a bit. He hadn't realized he'd taken a step forward until that moment.

Fuck. He was doing a terrible job at hiding his newfound attraction and attachment to the female who was, no doubt, watching everything unfold through the window.

"You should probably go," Colton said. His voice was calm, even, but his body language promised violence and pain.

The leader locked eyes with Colton for a few moments before gesturing to the crows in the trees. With an ear-piercing sound, the crows erupted into the sky, squawking as they flapped their wings and caught the wind.

"This was on your people. They attacked us. There was no issue before then. If I hear of any talk of retribution…"

"What? You going to call in a few more of your buddies to fight on your behalf?"

Jude did his best to contain his rage when the male's eyes flitted toward the cabin. His brows lowered then he slowly turned his attention back to Jude, a smile full of malice creeping across his face.

Fuck. Fuck fuck fuck.

He had to remain calm. He had to control his temper and his animal. He couldn't give this asshole a single inch or any reason to believe Scottie meant anything to anyone standing around.

His friends waited until the crows were long gone, sticking around to make sure they didn't circle back to attack when there were less males.

"Thanks for coming," Jude said, extending his hand to Gray.

"Any time, brother. You and your Flock have helped us plenty of times."

"The females," Jude said, narrowing his eyes as hazy memory came to him. "There were females missing. But not from your group."

Gray raised his brows and grinned. "You'll get there, brother."

The bears and wolves left, leaving Jude with his Flock.

Scottie stepped onto the porch, a thick sweater encasing her body. She gripped the sides and held it tighter around her body, staving off the cold air.

"You can ride back with me," Luca said.

Jude glanced back at Scottie.

"I'm going to stay the night. Make sure the crows don't return."

When he turned back to Luca, he rolled his eyes at the male who'd said he was the Second in command. Luca grinned knowingly, his eyes moving from Jude to Scottie and back again.

"Do you remember any of our numbers?" Luca said, and it sure as hell sounded like a teasing jab.

"I'll put your number in my phone," Scottie said as she stepped down from the porch.

She handed her phone over to Luca and waited as he programmed his number then handed it back.

"If there are any problems, give me a call. We'll get here as quick as possible," Luca said.

He waved the other hawks to follow. The trucks filed down the driveway, honking once before disappearing around the corner.

"I guess I should have asked if it's okay for me to stay before declaring it," Jude said.

"Of course it's okay," she said. She looped her arm through the crook of his elbow and led him inside. "You did good," she said.

"What?"

"I thought all you boys would end up in another fight on my lawn. You all behaved. Good job."

She winked at him when he glanced down at her.

Reaching over, he poked her in the ribs when he realized she was teasing him, then smiled at the squealed giggle.

It was music to his ears, a sound he wished to hear every single day.

The smell of pizza was in the air as they stepped through the door. "I got hungry, so I threw a pizza in the oven. That okay with you?"

He hadn't realized how hungry he was until she mentioned the food. His stomach rumbled and he smiled as he covered it with a hand.

"I should have fed you earlier."

"You really don't have to take care of me anymore. I'm okay now," Jude said, following her to the small kitchen and lowering onto the chair he'd sat in earlier in the afternoon.

"Sure I do. The outer wounds are healed, but your brain is still all jumbled. Do you have a headache or anything?"

He'd had a dull throb since he'd woken on the couch, but he shook his head.

"I'm really okay."

"Does that mean you no longer need a sponge bath?" she said with her back turned.

A surprised chuckle burst from his mouth. One day and she made him feel as though he'd been in this kitchen hundreds of times, made him feel as though they'd spent hundreds of afternoons together, made him feel as if, for once, he could finally be himself without judgment.

And he wanted her. He wanted her in a way he could only admit to himself. But not to her. Not yet.

She woke something inside of him, something other than his hawk.

Pushing to his feet, he moved to stand behind her. When she turned, her lips parted to say something, Jude dipped his head and claimed her mouth.

It was soft at first, tentative. But when her arms snaked around his neck, he tilted his head and deepened the kiss.

That was the moment he realized how fucking lost he was to Scottie. It was the moment he realized he would do anything and everything to have her in his life permanently.

Chapter Four

Jude's stubble scratched at the skin around Scottie's mouth, but she didn't care. The only thing that mattered was that he kept kissing her.

His tongue danced with hers, the velvety sweetness of his mouth mixing with the beer he'd drank at Skullbone territory. His arms moved around to her back and hugged her tightly to his hard body, his fingers splaying on the small of her back.

Too many clothes. There were way too many clothes separating them at the moment.

And then the stupid oven beeped that the pizza was done.

Pulling away, she realized she had seriously just contemplated ripping her clothes off and making love with Jude right there in the kitchen.

They'd known each other less than twenty-four hours, but it felt so much longer. He felt like an old friend, or…her soul mate.

Her cat purred at the thought. It appeared her animal was more than ready to claim Jude as her mate and mark him with her teeth.

She wondered if crows marked their mates. Their animals didn't have fangs like predator Shifters, but surely there was a way for flight Shifters to complete the changes that let the world know the female was officially off the market.

Jude's hands were firm as he gripped her hips, lifted her, and set her on the counter. He then rummaged through the drawers until he found an oven mitt and slid the pizza onto a plate.

"How hungry are you?" he asked, his voice deep and rumbly, the sound doing all kinds of yummy things to her body.

"What are we doing?" she asked from her perch on the counter.

Jude took a step back, his lips pink and kiss swollen. "I'm sorry. I…shit."

"Don't freak out. I just want to make sure we're not about to make a big mistake."

Pushing his fingers through his hair, he reached down and tried to hide the fact he was shifting his engorged dick to a more comfortable position.

"It wouldn't be a mistake to me," he admitted. "You don't want me?" he asked.

"Uh, hell yeah I want you," she said, her cheeks heating with a blush. "I just…we've known each other less than a day. And now we're moving closer to getting naked. And, to be completely honest with you, there's a real good chance my mountain lion will mark you."

She couldn't believe she'd admitted that out loud, but it was best to put everything on the table so they could both make the right decision about their lives and their futures.

Jude leaned forward, setting a hand on either side of her hips and trapping her on the counter. The way he inched closer, the way his glowing silver eyes bored into hers, set her blood on fire.

"I want you," he said, his warm breath fanning across her tingling lips. "My animal wants you. I know this is fast, but I don't give a fuck. I have never felt as comfortable around another person as I do with you."

"That you can *remember*," she said in an attempt to break the tension, but her voice came out breathy.

His lips quirked at the corners and his body shook lightly with a soft chuckle.

"That I can remember," he said, repeating her words. "I feel…it feels like you were meant to be in my life. Like I was meant to arrive on your porch—"

"Technically in my yard—"

"Like we were meant to meet. I…maybe it's too fast, but I truly believe you're it for me. You're the female I've looked for my whole life without knowing I was even searching."

His words warmed her heart. And mirrored her own feelings. She'd had no desire to form any connections or to insert herself in another person's life. Attachments always ended up in loss and pain.

Jude felt different. He felt permanent. He felt like a rock on a mound of sand.

Lifting her hand, she pressed her palm against his stubbled cheek. "Promise me this isn't a fling."

His brows lowered and his eyes lost a touch of their glow.

"I have never felt more certain about anything in my life, Scottie. You were meant to be in my life. I was meant to be in yours. This...pull between us feels like the mating bond. You're mine, Scottie. I'm yours. You can have me in any way you want, even if that means only friendship. But I want to be in your life. Permanently."

Again, he'd mirrored her thoughts.

Lunging forward, she threw her arms around his neck, wrapped her legs around his waist, and slanted her mouth over his with such need their teeth bumped. He chuckled against her mouth. But that chuckle quickly died when he lifted her with his hands cupping her ass and carried her from the kitchen.

When he stopped and pulled his mouth from hers, she frowned at him. "Why did you stop?"

His eyes were glazed with lust and glowing the most beautiful vibrant silver as he stared into her face. "Bedroom," he grumbled.

"That way," she said, pointing over his shoulder toward the short hallway.

The bed wasn't made, but the room was clean and tidy.

Jude didn't stop moving until his shins hit the mattress, nearly dropping Scottie before lying her on her back and following her down.

They were moving too fast. She knew that in her head. But her heart and body refused to listen to any voice of reason.

She wanted him.

Bull shit. She *needed* him. She needed the closeness and intimacy that would only come when their bodies were connected.

Scottie had warned Jude that her inner cat wanted to mark him. And he hadn't protested, hadn't told her he wasn't ready for something that profoundly deep and permanent.

Quite the opposite. He'd told her how important she felt to his life. He'd opened his heart and exposed his feelings to her with full vulnerability.

Her hands roamed his face, his neck, smoothed down his chest, until she reached the hem of his shirt and tugged upward. He pulled away only long enough for her to pull the shirt over his head and toss it to the floor beside her bed.

Jude immediately leaned back down, taking her lips in a hungry, desperate kiss that was filled with far more than pure lust. There were so many unspoken words in the way his mouth moved against hers, so many unshared feelings in the way his fingers skimmed her cheek and trailed down her neck to her shoulder.

When Jude pushed back from her, resting his weight on his forearms, he stared down her with such awe it took her breath away.

"You're so beautiful," he whispered in the dark.

The next time he pressed his lips to hers, it was gentle, soft, as though he was worshipping her mouth. His fingers skimmed across her shoulder blade and moved lower to cup her breast through her shirt and bra.

"Jude," she whispered against his mouth. "I need to feel you."

While their first moments had been rushed, Jude took his time to sit back on his heels and slowly peel the clothes away from Scottie's body like he was unwrapping a gift.

"Fuck, you're perfect," he said.

He didn't touch her at first, simply drank her in with his eyes.

And then he lowered his head and kissed the valley between her breasts, taking one mound into his hand to caress and squeeze while his lips trailed across the other. He sucked her nipple into his mouth, teasing and lapping at it, nipping it lightly with his teeth before soothing it with the flat of his tongue.

Lowering further, he kissed and nipped at her stomach and ribs, causing her to squirm when he hit a ticklish spot, then lowered his head until it was cradled between her thighs.

The moment his tongue swiped through her folds, she tossed her head back and moaned, the sound deep and guttural in the back of her throat.

Jude made love to her with his mouth, licking and sucking her clit until she was panting with the need for release. Pressure built low in her belly and exploded outward, sending fireworks off behind her closed lids.

She fell apart with his name leaving her mouth.

44

"Lose the pants," she ordered as he sat up and swiped the back of his hand across his mouth.

That deep chuckle rumbled from his chest again and sent another wave of need coursing through her. He was going to drive her crazy. One day together and she was addicted and knew she would never get enough of him, of his body, of the way he looked at her like there was no other woman on the planet.

His eyes stayed locked on hers as he pushed the sweats she'd bought him earlier down his hips. He hadn't bothered to change when they'd returned to his territory. As much as she tried to pretend otherwise, she felt a sense of pride that he'd chosen to continue wearing something she'd purchased for him.

The moment he was exposed, his cock jutted toward her and her mouth went dry. He was thick and long and so ready for her.

"Shit. Protection?" he asked. Neither could carry the types of diseases humans had to worry about, but pregnancy was a very real thing and not something Scottie was ready for just yet.

She was mildly embarrassed to admit she had a couple of condoms in her nightstand. But it wasn't like he was coming to her a virgin. No way could he think she would be, either.

Shimmying to the side, she opened the top drawer and rummaged through until her fingers found the foil wrapper, then handed it to him.

Jude ripped the container open with his teeth and rolled the latex over his length as Scottie watched, damned near panting with the urge to sit up and wrap her lips around him, to taste him, to take him into her mouth.

Kissing a path up her legs, he settled himself between her thighs, pressing a kiss to her lips as he reached between them and guided the tip of his hardness to her core.

They both moaned as he slid in slowly. Jude waited a moment, giving her body time to adjust to the invasion, then slowly withdrew and pushed into her again, building her need higher with each thrust of his hips.

While he'd started out slowly, the pace didn't remain that way. Within moments, he was pumping into her hard and fast. She raised her hips to meet him thrust for thrust, crying out and moaning as the pressure began to build again.

It was rare for her to find release once with a male, and now she was going to experience her second orgasm in one night.

Yep. Completely and unapologetically hooked on Jude.

His thrusts became frenzied. He sat back on his haunches, pushing Scottie's knees until they nearly touched her chest.

And then she fell apart.

There was no way she could hold back, no way she could contain the scream of pleasure that tore from her lips.

Just lasted a few more thrusts before he pulled from her, yanked the condom from his cock, and finished on her stomach with a primal growl.

Scottie had been able to refrain from Shifting her teeth and sinking them into Jude's shoulder. She'd controlled her urge to mark him before they were able to have a full and logical conversation about their future together.

Yet he'd marked her in his own way, by covering her with his scent.

He'd made it clear as day how he felt about her, about them, but saying it and following through were two different things. She'd experienced enough of that in her life, experienced abandonment by people who were supposed to care for her after so many loving words and promises.

Collapsing forward, Jude pressed his forehead to Scottie's shoulder as he sucked in breath after breath.

"Wow," she breathed out.

The mattress shook as he chuckled.

"Yeah. Wow."

She wasn't sure why she'd thought their first time would be awkward. But like the rest of the day, it felt as though their bodies knew each other, it felt as though their souls had united the moment he'd connected their bodies until they were one.

Scottie rested her head on Jude's shoulder. She'd fallen asleep hours ago, but Jude couldn't make his brain stop turning.

She was his mate. He'd known her less than twenty-four hours, but he'd never been more sure of anything in his life.

It didn't matter that he couldn't remember much from before this afternoon. It didn't matter that the names of his friends were still lost to him. What mattered was the woman in his arms.

Her hair tickled his chin when he turned his head to press a gentle kiss to her forehead.

He was the Alpha of Skullbone Flock. But he didn't want to leave Scottie's side. He didn't want to leave her bed or her house. And he wasn't sure she would be amenable to leaving her cabin to stay with him in his little home that had been built by his and his Flock's hands. It was barely big enough for him let alone all Scottie's belongings.

Perhaps he should wait to have that conversation until after his memory was fully restored.

As he gently ran his fingers through Scottie's long, dark hair, his eyes grew heavy and his thoughts grew fuzzy. It had been a long day. Definitely a surprising day. And had ended in the best way possible – making love to the most beautiful woman he'd ever laid eyes on and getting to sleep with her in his arms.

Jude woke with a start. Scottie had rolled onto her stomach, her face turned away from him, her hair splayed along the pillow. For a moment, her movement had startled him. It had been so damn long since he'd slept beside a woman.

Sitting up, he threw his legs over the side and stretched his back. Joints creaked and popped as he pushed to his feet and sought out the bathroom.

As he went through his morning ablutions, he found the toothbrush she'd bought him sitting on the vanity still in the wrapper. He should probably shower, but he wanted to stay covered in Scottie's scent a little longer. Since he didn't have fangs in his Shifter form, he couldn't mark her the way predators did to change the chemistry of her blood.

The best he could do was make sure she carried his scent with her any time she left the house.

Maybe that was a little much, but he wanted the world to know he'd found his true mate.

She could mark him, though. He actually thought she would have sunk her fangs into his flesh last night and was mildly disappointed when she hadn't.

But they had time. They had the rest of their lives for her to leave her mark on his shoulder.

He needed to call Luca. He needed to get hold of Big River and Blackwater to thank them for joining last night. He hadn't been sure what to expect, but after Clint was killed and the new Alpha of Black Feather, Dane, had taken over...

"Holy shit," he breathed.

Rinsing his mouth, he hurried from the bathroom and practically launched himself onto the bed, shaking Scottie awake with a hand on her shoulder.

She rolled onto her back and looked at him through sleepy eyes. The skin around her mouth was still red and irritated from his whiskers. He needed to shave as soon as possible. He hated to think he'd hurt her in any way.

"What's wrong?" she asked, rubbing the heels of her hands against her eyes.

"I remember. I remember everything," he blurted out as he knelt beside her.

"Really?" Her smile was sleepy but wide and genuine.

"I was in the bathroom brushing my teeth and remembered the name of the former Alpha and the current Alpha of Black Feather. I remember. Holy shit."

"That's awesome," she said, holding her arms out to him.

Jude practically laid on top of her and hugged her, lifting her from the bed and crushing her body to his.

Her hands suddenly pushed at his chest, shoving his weight from her.

"How do you feel about...us? About last night?"

"What do you mean?"

48

"Now that you remember your life, do you regret last night?" she asked.

"Hell no! I don't know why that question would even come to your mind."

Scottie pushed to a sitting position and leaned her back against the headboard. "I didn't know if you would suddenly remember you had a mate back home or something."

He huffed a laugh that sounded more like a snort. "I have never Claimed a woman before. I don't have a mate. You are the first woman I've ever met that I've wanted to spend my life with."

"Even though we barely know each other?"

Jude shrugged up his shoulders. "We've got plenty of time to get to know each other. You know the mate bond can happen fast. The rest will come with time."

"You mean love will come with time."

"Well, yeah," he said. How could she possibly question how he felt about her after the day – and night – they'd spent together.

Her smile was slow to appear but so sweet on her still kiss swollen lips.

"I need to get some work done today. It's technically a work day for me," she said on a yawn.

"You said you work from home. What do you do?"

"Build websites for people. Make graphics. That kind of thing."

He frowned. He hadn't seen so much as a laptop in the time he'd spent in her house.

"Other room," she said with a jerk of her head toward the door.

"Oh, now I'm curious."

He climbed off the side of the bed and hurried out of the room and across the hall. There was a fully furnished office in the spare bedroom complete with an array of computers and other gadgets for purposes Jude couldn't begin to understand.

"Wow," he said, stepping back into Scottie's bedroom. "You're the real deal."

"Yeah. A lot of years, a lot of training myself, and a lot of money went into that room."

"So, why do you live in this place?" he asked.

"What do you mean?"

She stood, and his body instantly hardened as she pulled clean clothes from her dresser and passed him on her way to the bathroom.

"I mean, why don't you live with a Pride? Or a bigger house?"

While she didn't say much at first, he noted the way her shoulders seemed to tense when he'd asked about living among a Pride. She didn't come across as shy; she'd had zero problems speaking with his friends yesterday.

So why did she keep herself so isolated?

"I like my house. I like being away from the noise and chaos of neighborhoods. And the property gives me plenty of space for my mountain lion to run without being spotted."

Mountain lions were fairly common in Missouri, but no doubt her animal would be much larger than her wild cousins like all other Shifters.

He couldn't help but notice she hadn't addressed his first question about forgoing living among a Pride.

He would let it go. For now. She obviously didn't want to discuss it and he wouldn't push her, not after everything she'd done for him yesterday.

She stopped in the doorway of the bathroom when he nearly followed her inside.

Smiling up at him, she said, "Were you planning to join me?"

Ohhh. So tempting. But he really needed to contact Luca and discuss the bullshit that had conspired yesterday.

"Do I want to? Absolutely. But I need to make some phone calls. Can I use your phone?"

"Of course. It's on the nightstand."

She tilted her head up when he lowered his to claim her lips in a quick kiss, then closed the door, leaving it open a gap.

He wanted to assume it was an open invitation. Not joining her was the hardest fucking thing he'd done in a long time. He so badly wanted to watch as she ran her hands over her wet, soapy body.

But until he learned whether or not Black Feather could be a threat to Scottie in the future, he had to keep his head straight.

Looking down at his body, he decided he really needed to put on some pants or he would continue walking around with a flesh and blood compass, one that was pointed directly toward Scottie.

After his ass and junk were covered, he lifted Scottie's phone from the nightstand and hit Luca's number that she'd saved last night.

They had a butt load to discuss, starting with whether or not Black Feather was a threat to Scottie and ending with whether or not the new Alpha needed to meet the same fate as the last.

Chapter Five

Scottie stepped out of the bathroom to find Jude pacing the living room with her phone pressed to his ear. Periodically, he would grumble a question or make a comment interspersed with angry or frustrated growls.

She'd dressed in the bathroom to avoid any further distractions – for either of them – but the towel was still wrapped in her hair.

As much as she would love to explore Jude's body some more, they had some things to discuss. He'd said he didn't regret what they'd done last night and that his feelings toward her or about them as a couple hadn't changed, but she needed to make sure before she allowed him into her heart any further.

But she wanted to. She wanted to trust in at least one person on this planet. She wanted to believe there was at least one person who would never walk away from her or leave her alone.

That would take longer than a single day, though. And a conversation about all the details like their living situation. She'd bought her house and property on her own after saving up for years. He was the Alpha of the Skullbone hawks and had a house in their territory.

Would either of them be willing to give up their home to live together? And would that end up being some kind of deal breaker?

She wouldn't know the answer to any of her questions until they had time to sit down and talk.

For now, though, she would let him figure out the issue with the crows. She still couldn't believe the crows had attacked the hawks midflight. It wasn't exactly outside of the norm for Shifter groups to fight, but it was far too risky to fly around in flocks as big as the one she'd seen yesterday. Had they ended up over a human's house…

With a shake of her head, Scottie slid her feet into her favorite house shoes and padded into her office. She'd get some work done while Jude talked to his people.

Flipping on the light, she crossed the room and pushed various buttons to power up her equipment. It was a fairly light day with only two orders for graphics, but both clients had requested images that would take her quite a bit of time to complete and perfect. She refused to send anything out until it was absolute perfection, and always offered changes if the client wasn't completely satisfied. Which was why she had so many repeat customers.

Once the screens all came to life and she had the appropriate programs and emails pulled up, she let her fingers do the rest. Her entire career had started and grown through self-education. She'd watched endless videos, taken online courses, and the rest was self-taught through trial and error.

Now? Now she had a successful company with a staff of one. She literally wore every hat for her little business and that was fine with her. It prevented her from having to do any face to face with anyone who might work for her and inadvertently outing Shifters when her eyes flashed or a growl bubbled up from her chest.

Besides, it was kind of nice to not have to wear suits or do her hair and makeup every day before working. Most days she wore comfortable lounge clothes or even pajamas while working.

Jude's voice rumbled through the door, rising occasionally before lowering to a threatening sound.

Was he still speaking with his Flock? She couldn't imagine Jude threatening his own people, especially not since he regained his memory.

As she positioned images in place and added text, she heard his heavy footsteps echo through the house until it stopped directly outside of her office.

He didn't say anything at first and she wondered if he was still on the phone. Turning to glance at him over her shoulder, she hit save so she wouldn't lose her place and swiveled the rolling chair to look up at him.

"Well?"

His heavy sigh told her more than words could. But he let her know he would be returning to his home today to get some things situated.

"Is everything okay?" *Is this the moment you realize you made a mistake?*

Crossing the room, he bent and pressed his lips to her forehead. "I think it was more fun when I didn't remember my role."

His words were meant to be funny, but she could hear the sadness in his voice and see it in his pretty gray eyes.

"The crows are threatening retribution for their fallen members."

Scottie frowned. "I thought they attacked your Flock."

"They did. We were checking things out, keeping an eye out for rogues, that kind of thing. We were ambushed. And you know the rest."

"That was risky."

"Yeah."

"So, if they started it…" She raised her brows at him with a shake of her head.

Another sigh escaped him as he crossed his arms. "I don't know. We don't have any females in our Flock, so we won't need to call in backup if they attack the territory. But if anyone is caught out alone, it could turn ugly."

"Did you talk to their Alpha?"

"Yeah."

She'd been right about his change of tone. "I take it by your scowl the conversation didn't go well."

He shook his head. His hand raised and his fingertips grazed her cheek. Pushing the hair from her face, he lowered his head and pressed a lingering kiss to her lips. "Is it okay if I come back later?" he asked when he pulled back.

"Uh, yeah," she said with as much *duh* in her voice as she could inflect.

The scowl smoothed and a smile bloomed on his face. His deep chuckle warmed her and caused butterflies to flap their wings like crazy in her stomach.

"Hopefully, it won't take long. My phone should still be at my house from before we Shifted so I'll call you if it starts getting late."

"It's fine. I work for myself. I can stay up or sleep in as late as I want," she said, hoping she didn't sound uber desperate. Because she badly wanted him to come back tonight to join her in her bed.

Well, that and so they could talk. But mainly because she wanted to feel his body again.

He smiled as he backed toward the door, his eyes glued to her face as though he didn't want to let her out of his sight any longer than he had to.

"I'll call you later," he said at the doorway.

"I'll be waiting," she said with a wink.

She really would love to spend more time with him today, but she had work to get done. It was better to stay on top of each order and job rather than to let them build up, even when her days were lighter.

When he finally backed through the door, Scottie listened to his heavy steps move through the house. The front door opened and closed.

Then opened and closed again.

His steps moved toward the room before his head peeked around the corner.

"I rode with you last night," he said with a sheepish grin.

Scottie chuckled and pushed to her feet. She'd forgotten all about that, too. She'd been so carried away with the events that had unfolded throughout the day and then the wonderful night they'd had that she'd completely forgotten that he didn't have a vehicle at her house.

"Guess Shifting and flying home wouldn't be such a great idea right now, huh," she teased.

Stepping into her bedroom, she kicked off the house shoes and slid her feet into a pair of sneakers then grabbed a hoodie and pulled it over her head.

Jude waited in the hallway, his hands shoved into the pockets of the sweats he still wore…and showcasing what she craved so much.

Scottie forced herself to keep her eyes on his face so as not to get distracted and make them both lose time in the day needed to complete their work and duties.

But at the end of the day, she had every intention of enjoying every inch of his body without the interruptions.

"Ready?" she asked.

"No," he said then shrugged.

She shook her head with a smile and passed him, grabbing her purse and keys from the table.

Jude stepped out first, his eyes going to the sky and trees surrounding her property. When he felt it was safe, he moved so she could step out behind him.

It was kind of comical to see his big body folded into her small sedan. But now that he'd recovered his memory, he could drive his own truck to and from her house. He could ride in comfort and come and go as he pleased.

Although, if she had her way, he'd stay more than leave.

It was probably way too early to think about things like cohabitation, especially since Scottie hadn't marked him yet, but she couldn't help it. She liked having Jude in her home. She liked having him in her space and in her bed.

Scottie had been to his territory last night but still needed him to guide her. She wasn't the greatest with directions. Why the hell did people say things like north and south? All they needed to tell her was whether she turned left at the light or right at a restaurant.

There were trucks and SUVs parked along the row of small houses. She wondered what the Flock did for a living but figured that was a discussion for another time. While they might not have house payments, surely, they had other bills, thus would have to have some form of income.

She just hoped they didn't make their money in an unsavory manner.

No way. She couldn't picture someone like Jude breaking the law. She couldn't picture him so much as jaywalking. There was something about him, something about the honesty and warmth in his eyes that told Scottie he was a good guy.

He undid his safety belt and leaned across the center console to claim her lips once more. This kiss was lingering, but he didn't tunnel his fingers into her hair or deepen the kiss, simply left his lips pressed against hers until her heart began to race.

Pulling away, he leaned his forehead against hers, his warm breath fanning across her face.

"I'll finish up as quickly as possible."

"Please do," Scottie said, no longer caring whether she sounded like a sex-crazed female. She wanted him. Each minute they spent together made her want him more.

As did her cat.

Scottie watched him push from his side of the car then watched his tight ass as he walked away, then she jumped and blushed hard when he turned and caught her ogling him.

One brow raised, he winked, then climbed his stairs two at a time.

Yeah. She wanted him. Badly. But her animal was growing unsteady the longer it went without sinking its teeth into Jude's shoulder.

Jude hated to do it, but he went straight to his pile of clothing and rummaged through until he found a pair of jeans and a sweatshirt.

Why did he hate to change clothes? Because the cotton was completely covered in Scottie's scent.

But so was his skin. Perhaps it was a little gross, but he had every intention of forgoing a shower until right before he had a chance to be with her so he could smell her all day.

The moment he sat on his futon to tug on a pair of boots, the thumping of feet echoed up the stairs and through his small, thinly walled house.

Luca pushed through the front door without knocking.

"Those fuckers were doing flyovers all night," he said without preamble.

"The crows? Are you fucking serious?"

Jude had attempted to talk some sense into the new Alpha, Dane, but it had apparently gone in one ear and out the other.

If the crows wanted a war, Jude would be more than happy to oblige. The Black Feather bastards had the numbers, but Skullbone had the size, fighting skill, and a lot of friends if shit got too hairy.

Luca paced the small one room house. The only section of Jude's place that had any privacy was his bathroom, and the door was nothing more than a curtain in case one of the other hawks happened to either step onto his porch or into his house while Jude was in there.

The Second in Skullbone glanced in Jude's direction, then did a double take. "What?" he asked.

"My brain is functioning again."

Luca's brows were high, but he nodded slowly. "That's...great. So, why are you smiling like a fool after I just told you the crows are fucking with us?"

Jude was smiling? He hadn't even noticed. One moment he was pissed about Black Feather, the next Luca was watching him like he'd lost his mind. Jude was still pissed. So why was his face not reflecting his thoughts?

Scottie. His short time with Scottie had done something to his heart and mind. And he sure as hell wasn't mad about it.

"Nothing. I was thinking about...something else."

"Or some*one* else," Luca said. His scowl smoothed and a smile slowly stretched across his face. "She seems cool. Chill. We all appreciate what she did for you. And for helping you find us."

"She's very cool. And very chill," Jude said.

He came just short of admitting to his Second that he was absolutely sure Scottie was the one person put on the planet for him, that she was his true mate.

Luca looked around Jude's place. "You'll have to build on. Or build a new place. None of our houses are big enough to add a mate."

Because none of them had found a female with whom they were interested in mating until Jude had woken on Scottie's couch. Up until that point, they had spent nearly all their time protecting as many innocent females of every species as possible. They helped their friends keep females safe, including their mates, and watched over the area. They kept an eye out for rogues or human traffickers.

Each of the hawks' homes were fine for a single person. But like Luca had said, there was no way two people could live comfortably in the four hundred square foot, one bedroom place without getting cabin fever or growing tired of looking at the other person when they bumped into them every time they turned around.

It was a conversation they hadn't had yet, but they'd really barely had time to talk about anything of true substance. All he knew was she felt as strongly for him as he did for her and that her mountain lion had an overwhelming urge to mark him.

Although it hadn't happened.

Hawks didn't mark their mates the same way the predators did, but that didn't mean he couldn't keep her covered in his scent at all times, even if it meant making love to her every time she planned to leave the house. And he couldn't care less how possessive that sounded even in his own ears.

Luca continued to watch him. "You don't think she'll move here, do you?" he asked.

Damn Luca. The males had been a part of the same Flock for so many years Jude's Second could read his thoughts simply by watching the changes on his face.

"I don't know. She seems happy in her home. And she has an extra room stock full of several computers and other…gadgets."

Luca's dark brows drew together. "What kind of gadgets?"

"Not the kind you're thinking, weirdo. She makes a living doing stuff on the computer; websites and that kind of stuff."

"Like I said, smart female. Earns money without immersing herself in the human world."

Jude nodded. Bending, he tied his boots and pushed to his feet.

"You ever think it would be so much easier if the humans knew about us?" Luca asked.

"Maybe if we'd been outed twenty or more years ago. Now…I can only imagine what they would do now. The human world seems to get scarier by the day. They might put their differences aside and declare war on our kind instead of each other."

Luca grunted. He waited for Jude to step outside then followed him onto the porch.

"Call a meeting. We got to figure this shit out. And I really don't like leaving Scottie unprotected if Black Feather are going to be acting like douchebags."

With a snort, Luca shook his head. "I have a feeling your female can handle her own."

She'd told Jude as much. And if she was a mountain lion, a flock of birds could only take her down if they showed up in force and dive bombed her enough to do damage to her eyes. Unless they attacked in their human forms and caught her off guard.

Jude's hawk stretched its wings in his head, determined to push its way to the forefront so they could return to their mate.

"I'm sure she can, too. And I know she'll bristle at the idea of a babysitter, but I'd feel better if someone hung around when I'm not there."

"Which I assume will only be while you're dealing with Alpha business."

There was no judgement in Luca's tone. He was merely stating a fact, that Jude would spend every waking second he could with Scottie.

"You assume correctly."

Luca veered off from Jude and went to the second house in the row, his knuckle rapping twice before he pushed through the door.

He continued down the row until all the hawks were circling the firepit. There were eight of them in this region, but several other hawks had split off from Skullbone in other areas while remaining loyal to Jude and the Flock, leaving only six in the territory. They aided each other when needed and had become strong allies in the sky.

"You good?" Burke asked as he lowered onto one of the chairs circling the cold fire pit.

"Right as rain," Jude said.

"He got his memory back," Luca said.

"I knew what he meant," Burke said with a roll of his gray eyes and a shake of his head. "Good to have you back. What's the plan?"

"That's why I wanted a meeting. We need to figure out how to back the new Alpha down while keeping Scottie safe."

Burke frowned over at Luca then his brows raised when realization hit him. "The chick from yesterday?"

"Yes."

"You like her?"

Fuck. He really didn't want to get into all that now. They needed to figure out how to neutralize the threat, but part of the reason he wanted everyone together was to figure out how to keep Scottie safe at the same time.

"Yeah. I like her. And I'm worried she'll be at risk since the dead crows were piled up in her yard."

"You think the crows will attack her?" Cohen asked.

Burke leaned forward and rested his elbows on his knees. "If Dane figures out Jude's attached to the female, he might fuck with her to fuck with him."

"That was my thought." Rather his *fear*. At the moment, it was his biggest fear.

"Want me to head over there?" Cohen asked.

He'd planned on waiting to ask any of his Flock to head to Scottie's until after they'd come up with a plan to back the crows down. But the longer he was away from Scottie, the more unsteady and unstable he and his animal grew.

"Yeah. I'd appreciate that."

Of the hawks, Cohen was an anomaly. While the bear Shifters tended to be fairly monstrous in size, hawks were lithe, leanly muscled instead of bulky.

Cohen was shaped more like one of the members of Blackwater Clan. Whether in his hawk or human form, the large male could hold his own long enough for Scottie to call Jude for help.

She had Luca's number, but it couldn't hurt to make sure she had the numbers of the other Flock members. His hawk hated the idea of any other male being the one to protect her, but his human side was aware another could get to her faster at times. He would gladly put his pride aside if it kept his mate safe.

With a curt nod, Cohen stood and grabbed the back hem of his shirt.

"Dude. Are you seriously going to strip right in front of us?" Burke teased.

"Drive there," Jude said. "Shift when you're closer so you'll have clothes if needed."

Because he did not want his female to see another dude naked, no matter how natural it was for Shifters to be nude on a regular basis.

Cohen stopped with his hand wrapped in the back collar of his shirt. His eyes narrowed, then his brows shot to his hairline.

"She's your mate," he nearly shouted.

A grin stretched across his face as he looked to each of the hawks sitting around in a circle.

Then his grin dropped so quickly his ears moved. "Wait…am I the last to know?"

"No. Pretty sure Luca is the only one who's caught on," Jude said.

While Cohen was the biggest and one of the fiercest fighters in the Flock, his brain also worked differently than the rest. The man could break down a strategy like no other, had the memory of a freaking elephant, but other things, like emotions, social cues, and sarcasm tended to elude him at times.

Honestly, Jude wasn't sure whether the others caught on, but he knew they could smell her scent all over him when they'd come close enough, even after he'd changed clothes.

"You do want me to stay hidden in the trees, though. Right?" Cohen asked.

"Right. I didn't tell her I was sending anyone over. I don't want her to Shift and attack you."

Jude had meant it as a joke, but Cohen looked incredibly serious as he nodded. "I'll stay hidden. She won't know I'm there until you want her to know."

Turning on his heel, Cohen lumbered off and stepped into his house. When he emerged, he carried his keys in his hand and hopped into his truck. The vehicle rumbled to life with a few chokes from the older engine.

They all watched as he backed out of his space and headed down the driveway, disappearing around the bend.

"No one's getting past that dude," Burke said with a chuckle.

"So, when's the wedding?" Luca teased.

"You done?" Jude asked.

They had business to deal with, but he didn't bother trying to hide his amusement at his friend's teasing.

"What's the plan, boss?" Burke asked.

"I'm going to attempt to have a sit down with Dane. In public. Have him meet me at Moe's."

"You think that's a good idea?" Burke asked.

"What the fuck is he going to try in a place full of our friends? He'd a dipshit, but he's not stupid."

"I don't think you should go alone," Burke said.

"Agreed," Luca said.

"If we go as a Flock, it might be perceived as an intimidation tactic or an act of war," Jude said.

"Good. Let that asshole be intimidated," Luca said.

He leaned back against the seat and crossed his ankle over his knee.

"I'd rather end this diplomatically, if possible. Avoid more bloodshed."

"They're the ones with lost crows. Not us," Luca said.

"You want to risk any of our Flock?" Jude asked.

There were far more numbers in Black Feather. While Jude's hawks could fight, each of them could be overpowered if caught out alone. It wasn't a risk he was willing to take, not with the people he was supposed to lead and watch over.

"At least take one of us," Burke said. "Alert him that you'll be bringing a witness and invite him to bring one, as well. Call Noah ahead of time to let him know your plans."

Luca smirked. "So he can call the bears and wolves and give them a heads up. I like the way you think."

"Not what I meant, but not a bad idea," Burke said.

Jude nodded as each male added their opinion, building a plan that would, hopefully, put this stupid rivalry to rest without another fight.

As soon as he was done with all this shit, he planned to pack an overnight bag and head back to Scottie's. They had a few things to discuss – like the fact he planned to have one of his hawks hanging around any time he wasn't able to be there to watch over her.

Already, he could hear her arguments. This might very well result in their first ever fight. And for some reason, he was more than excited about the makeup sex after.

He was a lost man.

Chapter Six

Scottie took a break from her work and pushed away from the L-shaped desk. Her stomach grumbled. She'd skipped breakfast and now she was starving.

Shuffling to the kitchen, she opened her fridge and bent to peer inside. She hated cooking solely for herself. It was boring and she always made way too much for one person. It would be so much better if Jude decided to stay with her as they grew their relationship and mating bond. Then she could cook for two, one of them being a large male who could put quite a bit of food away.

Or at least she assumed he would have the same increased appetite of every other Shifter she knew.

And once again she was back to wondering whether he would be amenable to leaving his Flock territory to stay with her. It was a lot to ask. She knew that. He was the Alpha of Skullbone. Did Alphas ever live outside of their group's territory? Would that be acceptable? Would his Flock still see him as in charge if he wasn't right next door?

More importantly, did he have any desire to live with her?

Just because they were mates, or at least agreed they'd both found the person made solely for them, didn't mean love would come immediately, any more than the desire to cohabitate would come any time soon.

She was getting ahead of herself. Scottie and Jude had known each other less than forty-eight hours. She hadn't marked him yet. They were merely getting to know each other, figuring out how they factored into each other's lives.

And then there was the whole hard-for-her-to-trust issue. She was trying her best to accept that not all people went away, but old beliefs were hard to dispel.

Rummaging through leftovers and take out containers, she settled on reheating some pasta from the night she'd met Jude. The night her life had completely changed. The night her yard was cleared of dead crows.

She leaned against the counter and waited as the microwave hummed. A loud screech filled the air. Jogging across the kitchen and living room, she propped her hands on the sill and looked through the window.

Squinting against the afternoon sun, she searched the trees, her heart thumping in hopes that Jude was back. Would he have flown, though? Or would he have driven?

If he'd flown, he would be naked when he floated to the ground and took his human skin back. She'd only bought a few pieces for him when he'd woken on her couch yesterday.

At first, she couldn't pinpoint the sound. But when the bird squawked again, she spotted it high in the trees, half hidden behind bare limbs.

As the microwave beeped, she pulled her phone from her pocket and dialed the only number she currently had – Luca's.

"Do you need Jude?" Luca answered.

"Is he there?" she asked.

"Is something wrong?"

"Is that Scottie?" she heard Jude say over the line.

There was a shuffling like the phone was being passed to a different set of hands.

"You okay?"

"There's a hawk in the trees outside my house. Not a wild one. Is he one of yours?"

"Uh…yeah. I was going to talk to you about that when I came over later."

She could almost picture him rubbing the back of his neck in discomfort as he answered her.

"Why would you send one of your hawks here? And why is he in the tree instead of coming to my door?"

"I figured he could keep an eye on you until I had a chance to talk to you about having a guard when I'm not there. At least until we get this crow shit under control."

After a few deep breaths, she reigned in her temper. "I've been protecting myself for a long time, Jude. Long before I knew you existed. Some birds aren't going to be a problem for my cat."

"A couple birds wouldn't be a problem for your animal. But a whole murder of crows could cause permanent damage to your eyes. Or worse. They could kill you before I could get to you."

The last few words felt as though they were being forced through his closing throat, as though the thought of her death restricted the air flow to his lungs.

"You could have given me a heads up. Or had him come to the door and introduce himself. It's weird having some stranger in the trees watching me like a creeper."

A huff of surprised laughter caused a staticky rush of air over the line.

"I didn't think of it like that. And I really didn't think you would notice him out there."

"He's not exactly quiet."

There was a beat of silence. "What do you mean?"

"He's been squawking off and on for the past ten minutes."

Another beat of silence. "Do you see anyone else out there? Any animals in the yard? Any other birds in the sky?"

She opened her front door and stepped onto her porch, hugging her sweater around her tighter. Using her free hand, she shielded her eyes from the sun and looked around, seeking anything out of the ordinary on her property.

"Not that I see. Why?"

"If he's squawking, he's either warning someone off or alerting you to something."

"Or he's alerting me to his presence," Scottie teased.

"Honestly, I wouldn't put it past Cohen to intentionally let you know he was out there."

"Cohen? Which one was he?"

She'd met six hawk Shifters last night, but not all of them had bothered introducing themselves.

"The big one."

She racked her brain. All the males were big. But there had been one of them who was built more like a predator Shifter than a flight Shifter.

"I think I know which one he was," she said. "Hey, Cohen!" she called out.

"What are you doing?"

"If you think I need a babysitter, there's no reason he needs to stay out in the cold until you get here," Scottie said.

"He's fine. And he'll be naked if he flies down to your porch now."

As he spoke, the hawk in question hopped from the tree limb and floated on the breeze, but circled around to the front of her house and disappeared.

"He left," she said.

Jude had said he was there for her protection, so she found it mildly confusing as to why he would disappear the second she let him know she was aware of his presence.

A few moments later, tires crunched on gravel.

"Did he drive here?"

"Yeah," Jude said. "I told him to drive then Shift. I didn't want him to walk around your property naked."

She chuckled. "Aww. Are you worried I might go buy him some new sweats, too?"

The deep rumble of Jude's laughter worked over the line and hit her right in the middle of her chest. Something about the sound of his laughter warmed her and caused a wave of affection to wash over her.

"Yeah. I don't want my girl spending her hard-earned money on anyone but me."

"Dude. Why don't you flirt with her on your own phone?" Luca said in the background.

"I'm going to call you from my phone so you have the number," he said, then ended the call abruptly.

Seconds later, her phone rang with an unknown number.

"You've reached your sugar momma," she teased.

It was so easy to play with him. They barely knew each other, had so many things they had to discuss before they could truly explore what was building between them, but everything felt easy with him, like an old friend.

If only all relationships could be so easy.

"You're a trip. Did Cohen come to the door yet?"

"No. He's sitting in his truck staring at me."

Jude made a sound in the back of his throat. "He's a little…different. Best guy you'll ever meet, though. Loyal. Wave him in. But make sure you set some boundaries or he'll invade your personal space at every turn."

"So…like a creeper?"

He chuckled again. "No. He just doesn't get some of the societal norms. That's all. But he's completely harmless, I promise. He'll keep an eye out for the crows until I get back. If you get tired of him being in your house, tell him I said to hit the trees."

"I'm not making him stay outside all day. It's cold."

"And he has feathers," Jude said.

"Hey, I have fur when I Shift and still don't want to spend the whole day out there."

They both went quiet a few moments. She didn't want to end the call. Even when Cohen ambled toward her, his eyes darting from her face to her feet and back again.

Male voices rumbled over the line.

"I gotta go. I'll call you as soon as I'm done over here. And I'm being serious – if Cohen gets on your nerves, tell him to go outside. He'll be fine. And call me if there are any problems at all."

"We'll be fine," she said, smiling at Cohen as he grew near. "But I will. Be safe."

"You, too."

And then there was that beat of silence again as though neither of them wanted to end the call or like one of them wanted to say more but knew it was far too soon to be whispering sweet nothings.

"Dude, just hang up," someone said from the other line.

"Bye, Jude," she said on a giggle.

Ending the call before he could say anything else, she craned her neck to look into Cohen's face. Now that they were standing feet from each other, she did remember him. He really was as enormous as she remembered.

"Hey," she said. "I didn't want you to think you had to stay out here all day. You can come in. It's too cold out here."

He barely met her gaze for more than a few seconds at a time, his eyes dropping to her chin, up to her forehead, even down to his feet.

"You weren't supposed to know I was here," he said, his voice deep.

Sucking her lips into her mouth to hide a smile, she jerked her head toward the door and led the way inside.

He closed the door behind him, but remained on the tiles of the entryway, his weight moving from one foot to the other like he was uncomfortable or nervous.

"Were you trying to let me know someone was on my property?" she asked.

His eyes rose to her face then darted away. "No."

"You were making a lot of noise. Jude thought you might be alerting me to danger or warning someone off."

"I...you weren't supposed to know I was out there. But I felt weird. I felt like a creeper hiding in the trees."

She barked out a laugh and pointed a finger at him, but dropped it when he frowned at her.

"Sorry. I'm not laughing at you. It's just that I told Jude you hiding in the woods was a little creeperish. So...thanks for giving me a heads up."

"You're welcome?" he said, his words sounding more like a question than a statement.

But he didn't move from his spot in her entryway.

"You can come in. Make yourself comfortable. Watch TV or whatever. I don't have a whole lot of snacks, but feel free to help yourself to anything in the kitchen. I need to get back to work."

Crap. She'd come out to eat lunch. The pasta she'd warmed would have cooled by now.

Hitting a minute on the microwave, she once more leaned against the counter while she waited for the beep to let her know she could finally eat lunch.

As she grabbed a fork from a drawer and found a can of soda in the fridge, she spotted Cohen slowly moving further into the living room until he lowered onto her couch. She'd thought her place felt smaller with Jude in it. That was nothing compared to how small and dainty her furniture looked with Cohen's huge body on it.

Smiling to herself, she carried her lunch into her home office and sat in front of the computers. She tended to multi-task, but today, she decided to eat and simply watch a video on YouTube instead of working.

Something was shifting inside of her, something was moving around and sliding into place, and she had a feeling it had everything to do with the big male who'd fallen from the sky less than forty-eight hours ago.

Jude sat a table, Luca on his right. A table in the far corner contained two bears from Blackwater Clan, the panthers and their mates from Ravenwood Pride, and wolves from both Big River and Morse Packs.

He still feared such a large presence could be misconstrued, but he also couldn't ignore his Flock's warning that Dane wasn't an honorable person and could very well show up with a large group.

Even if they stayed outside or took to the trees that surrounded the backside of Moe's Pub & Grill property, it would be far too easy for them to overtake Jude if he were to show up alone.

"You think he'll show?" Luca asked.

"He'll show. If for no other reason than to make a few threats," Jude said.

He rested his elbows on the table and cradled a cold beer between his hands. He hadn't taken so much as a sip from the bottle. He'd only ordered it to try his best to make the meeting at least *appear* casual. It was far too early to drink. At least for the middle of the week.

Thirty minutes after the time Jude had set for the meeting, the door to the bar opened and sunshine sliced across the wood floor.

The smell of fur increased as Dane stepped inside, followed by six of his crows.

Damn. He hadn't doubted Luca or any other members of his Flock, but hated when he was wrong. He'd really thought a fellow Alpha would at least respect a meeting in public, respect the only Shifter bar in the county.

He should have known better.

Any Alpha who would allow his members to attack another group unprovoked then have the balls to be pissed that Skullbone had dared protect themselves obviously wasn't an honorable male.

Jude and Luca stood as Dane approached. His crows took a table closer to the bar, giving the Alphas some space. Even Luca moved from the table and sat on a stool pulled up to the bar and chatted with Noah as he prepared orders.

"What?" Dane said the moment he was seated across from Jude.

"There is no reason our two groups need to be at odds. Flight Shifters are the minority in our world. My people have no –"

"You stacked my men up like garbage in that female's yard."

At the mere mention of Scottie, Jude's hawk ruffled its feathers and began to watch his enemy closely.

Dane leaned against the back of his chair, crossed his arms over his chest, and narrowed his eyes at Jude.

"The female means something to you. Is that why you hid the bodies in her yard?"

Had Jude been a predator Shifter, his eyes would have flashed with a bright glow and a growl would have rumbled from his chest. It was one of the good things about being a flight Shifter – it was easier for his kind to blend into human society.

"The bodies were not hidden. We called you to retrieve your fallen members. The same members who attacked my Flock unprovoked. And the female was nothing more than an unfortunate bystander."

"Then why are you covered in her scent?"

Jude *sensed* more than *saw* his friends bristle and pay closer attention. Though he wasn't sure whether they were watching to take

71

out Dane or to keep Jude under control if he were to lunge across the table in an attempt to remove the fucker's head from his shoulders.

Jude's nostrils flared as he inhaled deeply then blew it out slowly. He would not let this asshole goad him into a fight. That would result in a brawl in the middle of his friend's bar.

"The female had nothing to do with your people's attack, she had nothing to do with their deaths. She simply lived in the area where we happened to be surveilling. If anyone so much as flies within a mile of Scottie's property—"

He cut himself off the moment he realized he'd used her name. Fuck. Luca had been right – this had been a terrible fucking idea.

The only reaction from Dane was a raised brow. A muscle jumped in his cheek as he continued to glare at Jude.

"Who killed my people?"

"I don't know. When they attacked, my Flock simply defended themselves. When it was evident they were there for more than simple irritation, we fought back. Lives were lost."

"*Crow* lives were lost. It seems odd to me that you didn't lose a single member of your tiny Flock," Dane said.

Jude shrugged up his shoulders. "My men are better fighters."

That muscle jumped in his cheek again as he glared at Jude.

"I want this to end now. I want this over before we walk through that door," Jude said with a jerk of his chin toward the exit.

Dane said nothing.

"There has to be a compromise. My men don't want another fight. They were attacked unprovoked but are willing to forget it happened if your crows will stand down. Any further attacks will be seen as an act of war and I will be forced to take action."

"That sounds like a threat," Dane said.

"Not a threat. We're both Alphas. We are both charged with protecting and leading our people. That includes doing what is necessary to keep any enemy groups from trespassing on our property – including in the air – or coming after my people. *All* of my people."

Jude might have been the Alpha of Skullbone Flock, but he would protect any of his friends as well as their mates and children.

It was a few more moments before Dane reacted at all.

72

With a curt nod of his head, he stood and headed toward the door. His Crew stood and followed him out but not before giving the room a glare as though they were at all intimidating to a room full of predators.

"That went about as well as expected," Luca said.

He rejoined Jude at the table, carrying his beer over and setting it on the table.

"He didn't agree to anything."

"No. He didn't," Jude said.

He clenched his teeth and inhaled deeply. This was far from over. It was obvious Dane was no different than the previous Alpha. The crows would attack again. There would be more fights. There would be a war.

But what really had his feathers ruffled was the fact Jude had dropped Scottie's name. Why the fuck had he opened his big mouth? He had inadvertently put his mate directly in the crosshairs of Black Feather's Alpha.

"I need to get back to Scottie's," Jude said, standing so quickly his chair almost tipped.

"Cohen is still there," Luca said.

He was attempting to comfort his Alpha, but Jude needed to be the one to keep his mate safe. And she was absolutely, one hundred percent without a doubt, Jude's mate, with or without the mark.

"From here out, I don't want Scottie left unprotected. If I have to leave for any reason, I want one of you to watch over her."

"We can help," Colton from Blackwater offered.

"You have two toddlers at home. The last thing you need to concern yourself with is me."

"I didn't specifically say me. I said *we*, as in your friends. As in the Clan, the Packs, and the Pride," Colton said with a smirk.

The males sitting at the table nodded with varying looks of determination on their faces. None of them could fight the crows in the sky, but they could keep Scottie safe, keep her protected, keep her from being pecked to death by a murder of psychotic crows.

"Thank you," he said as his throat tightened.

He wasn't sure whether it was fear or emotion keeping any more words from leaving his mouth. But it didn't matter. He had a group of friends who were fiercely loyal, who would help keep Scottie safe at all times.

"There is another option," Luca said. "She could always stay in our territory."

"It wouldn't work. She has a whole room of techy stuff. And she'll need to keep working. No way that stuff could fit in my place."

And they had no empty homes for her to use as a temporary office until they figured out what Black Feather's Alpha had planned.

"I'll stay with her as much as possible. We'll stick to the original plan of having someone step in when I have to leave. As long as everyone is amenable to that," Jude said.

Luca opened his mouth, but it was Brax from Ravenwood who spoke up. "I know Campbell has been looking for a fight. We'd be happy to hang out."

Brax had mated with a human who'd been hunting and executing rogues since long before the two had met. She was a badass little human who never shied away from a fight and appeared to have no fear and gave zero fucks about what anyone thought about her stepping up to a Shifter – male or female.

"Peyton, too," Tristan, the quiet member of Big River, spoke up.

Tristan's mate, Peyton, had been turned by an asshole who'd forced an animal inside of her. Her wolf had nearly taken Peyton's life during her first Shift. And ever since that day, her animal was not only somewhat unstable, but behaved as though she were the champion for anyone she felt was innocent or vulnerable.

Jude had never liked the idea of females fighting grown male Shifters. But the females he'd befriended over the years were all as fierce of fighters as their mates. They not only held their own in the many fights they'd all endured over the years but had bested most of their foes without any help from a male.

So could Scottie. At least that's what she'd told Jude. She'd told him her mountain lion was scrappy, that her inner beast was always up to a good fight. And he believed her. But he also knew people like the crows didn't fight fair.

He would stick to his plan for now, until they figured out whether or not Black Feather's Alpha would respect Jude's call for a truce.

And, honestly, he liked the idea of spending nearly every waking minute in Scottie's presence, even if she was in the other room working.

Chapter Seven

It was the fourth day that Jude had had to leave and sent someone to stay with Scottie. Not just anyone; each time, it had been Cohen.

At least the big male was no longer sitting on her couch and staring at the wall. He'd finally gotten comfortable enough to flip on her TV. He'd even rummaged through her kitchen for snacks once.

Why it was always Cohen, she didn't know. But it was fine with her. She'd grown comfortable around him, too. They didn't talk much, but he was warm and sweet and kept his distance from her.

And he still barely made eye contact with her.

After a few short conversations with him, she began to wonder if Cohen's brain wasn't wired differently. He was highly intelligent, but somewhat awkward during their chats, like he wasn't sure how to participate in small talk.

But *whew doggy*! The moment she'd complained about some issues she was having with one of her computers, he'd opened up and rambled things that would make most people's brains bleed. The male knew about computers even though he didn't own so much as a laptop.

She liked him. She'd only briefly met the others once more since the first day when Scottie had taken Jude to his territory in hopes of figuring out who he was and what his role was in the Flock.

Jude had also brought a few changes of his clothing and some personal toiletries to her house in that time. He refused to leave her alone for even a minute. Scottie wasn't some damsel in distress, but it seemed to make him feel better so she acquiesced to his request.

And it had been a request, albeit it a very thinly veiled request that bordered on a demand. She knew he would have someone in the trees even if she said no to a permanent sentry.

It was fine. Cohen wasn't an imposition. He didn't interrupt her day at all. And he'd only eaten a couple apples for a snack. Not like he was eating her out of house and home or playing the television too loudly while she tried to work.

Pushing her chair away from the line of computer screens, she pulled her arms over her head and stretched her neck and back. It might be time for her to invest in a new chair. This damn thing was killing her back and made her booty hurt after sitting in it for so many hours.

The front door opened and closed and Jude's unique scent made it to her office.

With a smile on her face, she swiveled the chair and turned toward the door, anticipating his appearance with butterflies in her stomach.

She still hadn't marked him. Her cat was growing impatient. It needed to happen sooner rather than later or there was a chance her beast might push forward and take matters into her own hands.

"Hey," she said with a grin when he poked his head around the corner.

"You busy?"

"I was just taking a break."

He entered her home office and crossed the room, his muscular legs eating up the space between them in long strides.

She stood and stepped into his arms as he extended them and tilted her face up for a kiss.

"Any luck?" she asked.

The hawks had been out doing their best to track the movements of the crows while staying as far under the radar as possible. As far as she'd been told by Jude – and she knew he was withholding things from her – there had been nothing to indicate they were a threat any longer.

Scottie wasn't so sure. She might have been ordered to stay inside of her cabin while the crows had gathered their fallen people, but she'd heard the conversation clearly. The Alpha of the crows had made it sound like she was a part of the death of the crows. They'd implicated that she was as much at fault as the hawks.

Which, of course, was utter and complete bull shit. She would have much rather had a nice, quiet, cozy day on her couch like she'd planned.

But had her nice, quiet, cozy day happened, she would have never met Jude. She would've gone years, or even her entire life, without finding her mate, her *true* mate, the one male the universe had sent just for her.

77

She wasn't one to believe there was literally only one person out there for each on the planet. She'd heard stories of Shifters losing their mate then finding another mate years later.

But she always wondered if the connection was as strong with the new mate as it was with the former.

He groaned in frustration. "They're up to something."

Her brows rose high. That was the most he'd revealed to her since that fated day.

"What makes you think that?"

"They've stuck close to their territory, haven't shown their faces at Moe's…crows don't tend to stay in one place long. They're definitely up to something. My money is on the Alpha planning something, something big."

"You're worried."

He scoffed and moved so he could lean his hip against her desk. She cringed when her computers wobbled. There was a whole lot of money sitting on the cheaply made desktops and his weight could cause the entire thing to topple.

"Not about me. I'm worried about you. And my friends."

"You think they'll use me to punish you?"

His shoulders rose and fell.

"I wouldn't put it past the Alpha or his Crew."

Scottie pulled her feet onto the chair and tucked them under her, then tightened her long, thick cardigan around herself. "You realize the cat always wins in a fight against a bird. I'm the last person you need to worry about."

"And I've told you those assholes don't fight fair. They won't come at you one at a time. They'll attack you as a group, try to blind you with their beaks and claws. And then I'll have to burn their entire territory to the fucking ground."

A smile tugged at the corners of her lips.

"What's so funny?"

"So big and protective. Kind of hot when you turn into a bodyguard."

His smile was reluctant at first, but he couldn't hold it back. With a shake of his head, he straightened and crossed the room.

"Mind if I make something to eat?" he asked, stopping at the doorway.

"Of course. But we're going to have to make a grocery run soon. I'm not used to cooking for more than one person."

"I got it," Jude said. "I'm eating way more than you. I mean, way more food than you eat."

He winked before disappearing down the hallway, leaving Scottie sitting there with hot cheeks and warmth pooling low in her belly.

The things that male did to her with nothing more than words or a look.

It had only been six days, yet she was growing more and more attached to him and could already feel her heart warming toward him. She knew it wouldn't be hard to fall head over heels for Jude, nor would it take long. Unlike humans, the knowledge that a Shifter had found his or her life mate came almost immediately. Love sometimes took longer, but still happened fairly quickly.

Honestly, she didn't care what humans or other Shifters did. All she knew was Jude was quickly growing as important to her as her next breath.

Turning back to her computers, she did her best to refocus on her work. The front door opened and closed again, but the television show never changed.

Rolling backward still seated in her chair, she leaned backward and peered into the living room. Cohen still sat on the couch, his big, sock covered feet propped on the coffee table.

"Hey," she said.

His head whipped around.

"Did Jude leave?"

Cohen nodded. "Food run." Then he turned back to the show.

Scottie didn't know if it was because he didn't want to miss anything or if, like usual, he had a hard time maintaining eye contact with her for more than a few seconds at a time.

"Food run as in junk food?"

"Groceries," Cohen said without turning around.

Staring at the back of Cohen's head another moment or two, she rolled her chair back to her desk. When she'd said they would need to get groceries soon she hadn't meant that moment.

And he'd stayed true to his word and refused to leave her alone even for the short time it would take for Jude to fill a cart with groceries.

By the time Jude returned, Scottie was hitting save on her work and emailing a proof to one of her clients.

Bags rustled and cabinet doors opened and closed.

Powering down all her computers, she pushed to her feet, stretched like a cat, then headed to the kitchen.

"What did you do?" Scottie asked as she surveyed the dozens of bags littering her counters and kitchen table.

"We needed food. And if my Flock will be staying here periodically, I'm responsible for feeding them."

He hadn't only bought staples like milk, bread, and eggs. He'd bought fresh fruit and vegetables, several packages of lunch meat, ground beef, chicken breasts, bags and boxes of snacks…

Scottie couldn't get through this much food in a month. Hell, it would take *several* months to get through it all unless she wanted to pack on a few pounds by munching on all the snack cakes, ice cream, cheese crackers, and the like.

"It's too much," she said with wide eyes.

"Eh. You know we eat a lot. And this way, you won't have to spend your money on my Flock or friends."

She still didn't know what he or his people did for a living. Perhaps that was something she should know about the male she planned to spend the rest of her days with, but it simply hadn't come up yet. Besides, it wasn't like he'd asked her for any money. She figured as long as he wasn't doing anything illegal or unscrupulous, it didn't matter how he earned his money.

But, yeah, she should probably ask eventually.

"What do you want for dinner?" he asked as he continued to put everything away.

"I don't know. I haven't really thought about it."

And now that there was so much laid out in front of her, she couldn't settle on one single thing. Everything looked so good.

Gripping her by her shoulders, he turned her and swatted her on the ass.

"Go relax. I'll cook dinner."

"Wow. I didn't know I was getting a chef as a mate," she teased.

Cohen stood and dipped his head.

"Where you going?" she asked.

"The Alpha is here. You don't need me anymore."

Scottie frowned at him. "Just because Jude's here doesn't mean you can't join us for dinner. In fact," she said, turning to look at Jude, "why don't you call the rest of the Flock and invite them over?"

Jude looked around her kitchen then the living room.

"You don't really have enough room for everyone to join. We'll have a cookout when it's warmer." He chose what he would cook and started searching for cooking utensils. "But Cohen can stay if you want."

The big Shifter was quiet, but she really liked him. He felt kind of like a little brother...even if he had over six inches on her and at least a hundred pounds.

"You sure?" Cohen asked.

"Absolutely," Scottie said. "Let's veg out while we wait for Jeeves to fix us dinner."

Jude chuckled as Cohen sat back down and Scottie curled up against the arm of the couch. She only barely paid attention to whatever show Cohen was watching.

She was far too interested in watching her mate move around her kitchen.

It was that moment she realized she wanted him there permanently. It was also the moment she realized she wouldn't move to his territory and prayed it wouldn't be a deal breaker.

Jude sat on the couch, his arm wrapped around Scottie as she snuggled up against his side. Her legs were on the cushions, a blanket draped over her.

Cohen had left immediately after eating, thanking Scottie for the invite before ducking through the front door.

The big male was quiet and a tad shy with new people, but he appeared to have taken a liking to Scottie. Jude wasn't sure he'd ever seen Cohen so comfortable with someone outside of the Flock and it made Jude warm to Scottie all that much more.

Scottie yawned and nuzzled closer to Jude, draping an arm over his stomach and hugging herself closer to his side. He was sure she would climb onto his lap if they could both comfortably see the movie they were watching.

"You tired?" he asked.

He lowered his head and pressed a kiss to the top of her head.

"Yeah."

For almost a week, he'd hoped and wished she would mark him. The lack of a mark didn't change his growing affection for her, but this was a primal need deep inside of him to carry a permanent reminder to any who saw it that she belonged to him. *He* belonged to *her*.

Waiting for her to untangle her limbs from him, he stood and wrapped an arm around her shoulders, walking with her to her bedroom.

She'd insisted the night before it was *their* bedroom, but he still hadn't brought up the subject of where they would live.

Everyone in the Flock knew there was no way she could fit all her computers into his home. But he was the Alpha of Skullbone and needed to be near his people. He had a feeling she wouldn't be hip on the thought of moving all the houses onto her property.

He bit back a chuckle as images of tiny homes dotting Scottie's lawn came to mind. If she asked what he was laughing at, he would have to be honest. And that would open up the conversation he wasn't sure either of them was quite ready to approach.

Why was he being so shy about this? The mate bond was unbreakable. They both felt it, both felt the pull, both felt the undeniable tether that bound them for life.

As she changed from the clothes she'd worn through the day into a pair of sleep pants and a tank top, Jude watched her and waited. Was she too tired? Would him bringing up this conversation stress her or scare her away?

And was he simply looking for yet another reason to avoid this conversation?

"Why haven't you marked me yet?" he blurted before he lost the courage or really gave his brain time to work up a more eloquent way of asking.

Tugging the hem of her tank top down, she turned and frowned at him.

"Why haven't *you* marked *me*?" she asked.

"Flight Shifters don't mark in the same way as predator Shifters."

She crossed her arms under her breasts, and it took nearly every ounce of his control to keep his eyes on her face.

Scottie continued to watch him, her lips pursing as she narrowed her eyes.

"I don't want to move," she said softly.

He'd assumed as much but had tried to find a way that they could both stay in Skullbone territory. She'd bought her house and her property all on her own. She didn't live within a family Pride.

Which begged another question...

"Why did you leave your Pride?"

He hoped and prayed she didn't tell him there was a male who'd broken her heart or that she'd endured abuse at the hands of the people who were meant to love and protect her. He'd heard stories of that type over and over again and wasn't sure he could keep himself from hunting down anyone, male or female, who'd hurt his mate.

"There was nothing there for me," she said.

"What do you mean?"

Her narrow shoulders rose and fell before she sat on the edge of the bed, her arms still crossed.

"No one stays. People don't stay. My mom died. My dad found another mate and moved away without a backward glance. Over and over, my friends moved away, leaving me there with people I barely knew. There was no reason for me to stick around."

No one stays. People don't stay.

Had she not marked Jude for fear he would walk away? Did she think that was even possible? Had he not shown her how much she meant to him even after their short time together?

Closing the space between them, he knelt in front of her, pulling her arms free so he could hold both her hands in his own.

"I'm not going anywhere. I would never leave your side...unless you wanted me, too," he said with a sheepish half smile. "I would never leave you, Scottie."

She blinked a few times as though she were keeping tears at bay.

"Is that why you haven't marked me?"

She turned her hands in his so she could grip his fingers. "That and the fact you'll have to leave your Flock. Alphas stay in their territory. I really don't want to leave my house. And there really isn't enough room here for all those big guys." She forced a smile, but it didn't reach her eyes.

"So what if Alphas usually stay in their territory. Not like it's a hard and fast rule. And if the Flock doesn't like it, I'll hand my duties over to Luca. I'm sure he would love to be Alpha."

"I could never ask you to do that," she said, gripping his hands tightly.

"You didn't ask. I offered. I would do anything to have you and keep you in my life, Scottie. If that means abdicating my role, so be it. Not like I was put in that position by choice. The title was more or less assigned to me when no one else stepped up."

Her body shook slightly with a soft chuckle.

"I don't think I would ever want that responsibility. Always the one everyone looks up to when crap goes sideways."

Like when he'd woken with zero memory of who the hell he was yet the Flock still looked to him for answers for what to do about the crows.

Scottie looked into his eyes, her golden-brown eyes flashing lightly for a brief moment as they lowered to the spot where his neck met his shoulder – the spot where she would sink her fangs into his flesh to mark her as his.

Her eyes sliced back up to his and she nodded slowly. "Okay."

84

"Okay?"

"We agree that we'll live here? And you promise not to walk away?"

"I would never walk away from you, Scottie. I couldn't. It would shatter my heart to pieces and rip my soul apart. And, yes, I would be honored to stay in your home."

"The Flock won't like it," she said.

Jude dismissed her comment with a grunt. "They'll get over it. If they're not content with their Alpha living elsewhere, someone else can step up."

"You really don't mind? You don't care about giving up your status?"

He pushed to his feet and sat beside her, turning her so she had to face him. "I care about you. I care about us. I care about completing our bond and, someday, maybe having a family of our own."

Scottie's eyes dipped to his shoulder again then up to his face.

Grabbing the back hem of his shirt, he tugged it over his head and tossed it across the room.

Her lips twitched as she tried to hold back a smile.

Holding up a finger, she pointed it toward the shirt lying on the floor. "We need to set a few rules if we're going to live together, starting with dirty clothes going in the hamper."

A smile stretched across his face. Leaning forward, he pressed his lips to hers, gently at first. But when he began to pull back, her hand raised and rested on his neck, holding him in place.

Her lips molded around his then parted, the tip of her tongue teasing the seam of his mouth.

With a moan, he opened for her, tasted her, reveled in the velvety sweetness of his mate's kiss. Jude wrapped his arms around her waist and dragged her closer until she threw one leg over his lap and straddled him.

The moment their bodies touched he was instantly hard. Then again, he was pretty sure he'd walked around with a constant boner for days. And had a feeling it would be a long time before he was able to be anywhere near his mate without wanting to have her beneath him.

Her small hands cupped his face as she tilted her head and deepened the kiss further.

Smoothing his fingertips over her spine and down her back, he cupped her ass and urged her to move, to grind against his rock-hard cock. There was no way he would deny her anything. Literally anything. He would walk away from his role as Alpha, he would move his belongings into her house and abandon his home in Skullbone territory.

He would give his own life for her. Anything to keep her safe and happy.

Scottie pulled away only long enough to pull her tank top over her head and tossed it in the same direction where he'd dropped his shirt. Later, he would tease her about missing the hamper.

But for now, he simply enjoyed the feeling of her full breasts against his chest, the warmth of her against his body.

Lie. Or at least half-lie. He could enjoy the way her tits felt against his hard chest while he was inside of her, while she rose and fell on his cock, riding him until they both found their release.

Chapter Eight

He said he wouldn't leave. He'd promised he would never walk away from her.

Scottie knew her deep seeded fear that everyone would one day abandon her was irrational and a touch childish. But after so many years of watching person after person leave her life, it was hard to erase that fear.

But she believed Jude. She believed him when he'd said he would be at her side for as long as she would have him.

He'd asked why she hadn't marked him yet.

She hated that his kind didn't mark their mates, hated that she wouldn't permanently carry his scent in her blood like other females who'd found their true mates.

There were other ways for her to carry his scent, though. And there had to be another way for the world to know her heart belonged to him as his belonged to her.

Lifting her hands, she scraped her nails against his scalp and ran her fingers through his silky, shoulder length hair. She'd never thought she would be attracted to a man with longer hair. But it was perfection on him. It lent an air of beauty to his rugged good looks. He was beautiful in a masculine kind of way.

And sexy as hell.

His hands gripped her ass and urged her to move. Not that she needed any urging. She could feel the hard length of him through his jeans and the thin material of her pajama pants.

Jude lowered his head and pressed kisses from her jawline to her shoulder blade, between her breasts before turning his head to take one pebbled nipple between his lips. He sucked and nipped at it gently with his teeth before soothing it with his tongue, drawing a shaky gasp from her throat.

"Jude," she whispered.

She needed him. She needed him closer. She needed to feel his bare skin against hers, to feel him deep inside of her.

But she couldn't do that when both were wearing pants.

Pulling from him reluctantly, and smiling when he groaned his disappointment, she pushed her pajamas to the ground, hooking her panties at the sides and pushing then down her legs, as well.

Then, she did something she'd fantasized about doing since the first time they'd slept together. She lowered to her knees between his thighs and worked at popping the button on his pants, then pulling down the zipper.

He leaned back and lifted his hips so she could work the denim down his hips where she let them pool at his ankles.

And then he was fully bared to her, his thick, silky length begging to be touched.

Wrapping her fingers around the shaft, she raised her eyes to his face as she lowered her head and took him into her mouth.

Jude's eyes rolled into the back of his head a second before he dropped his head back with a soft moan.

She took him into her mouth slowly at first, reveling in the taste of him, the feeling of his velvety soft skin against her tongue, growing addicted to the sounds he made as she ran her tongue along his length.

One hand wrapped around his cock, she let the other smooth up his bare thighs then up to his abs. The muscles bunched and quivered under her touch.

And then his fingers wrapped tightly in her hair and pulled her away.

"You have to stop or I'll finish before I have time to feel you clench around me," he said, his voice deep, guttural, full of lust and need.

Lifting her with ease, he nearly tossed her onto the bed, then kicked his pants the rest of the way off before settling between her thighs.

His hand moved to grip his cock and guide it to her core. The moment the flared head brushed against her she sucked in a breath.

"I need you," she nearly begged.

Slowly, he pushed into her inch by agonizing inch until he was fully sheathed deep inside of her.

But then he didn't move again. Simply stayed buried inside of her and lowered his head to claim her lips.

She needed him to move. Needed friction. Needed to feel his length rubbing all the deliciously sensitive places inside of her.

"Please," she whispered against his lips.

She felt his smile spread as he continued to kiss her, but he finally moved. Slowly at first, taking his time, one arm holding his weight from her while the other smoothed over her shoulder before moving down to cup one of her breasts.

"You're so fucking beautiful," he said against her mouth.

She knew he was going slow to make their time together last, knew that her mouth had pushed him close to the edge.

But she needed more. Needed him to push into her harder, faster. Needed...all of him.

Before she had any time to think, her mountain lion pushed forward and Shifted her teeth, causing her gums to throb and ache.

Lifting her head, she immediately latched onto his shoulder, nearly orgasming at the taste of his blood as the coppery warmth filled her mouth.

He grunted with both pain and pleasure.

When she pulled her teeth free from his flesh and lapped at the blood seeping from the punctures, he pushed onto his haunches, gripped her hips to raise them, and began pumping into her hard and fast.

As her breasts bounced and the mattress squeaked below her, her release built quickly and exploded so hard it stole her breath. She wasn't sure she'd ever come so easily with a man.

Everything about her time with Jude was easy. Everything felt so perfect, so natural.

And she realized, after such a short time, love was already blooming for him. She was already falling in love with him, and she couldn't find an ounce of doubt nor the urge to ponder the absurdity of it.

All she could feel was pleasure. All she could feel was Jude.

All she wanted was Jude. More time with him. More time in bed with him. More time on the couch with him. More teasing and laughing and smiling.

All she wanted was a life with Jude. And she realized she didn't care whether they had to find a way to make her computers fit in his territory or they stayed in her house or moved to a completely different area. As long as they were together.

Jude's thrusts became hurried, frenzied, desperate. His eyes flashed a mesmerizing silver, just the slightest hint of a glow.

This moment…her entire life felt as though the world shifted below her feet, as though the entire planet had been knocked from its axis and life as she knew it would look completely different by morning.

Scottie watched as Jude threw his head back with a grunt, then pulled free from her, shooting hot jets onto her stomach until he collapsed forward, his warm breath ruffling her hair and tickling her cheek.

Her own breath came in pants as her heartbeat struggled to return to a normal pace.

"Are you okay?" she asked when he didn't move.

Raising his head, he frowned down at her, his beautiful gray eyes still holding a touch of their silver glow.

"I'm amazing."

"Does it hurt?" She gently ran her fingertips over the raw punctures on his shoulder.

His head wagged slowly side to side.

He dipped his head and pressed a soft kiss to her forehead, the tip of her nose, then to her lips before finally rolling onto his side, dragging her with him so she rested her head on the crook of his shoulder.

"We should probably shower," she said.

She was lifted from the mattress and into Jude's arms so quickly she squealed with surprise, then giggled the entire way to the bathroom.

He washed his release from her stomach, then groaned when she took the bar of soap, lathered up her hands, and ran them over his body slowly.

"You're killing me."

With a laugh, she pushed him under the spray to rinse the suds from his body, then ended the shower with a squeak of the pipes.

They each claimed their own towels, then shuffled sleepily and naked to the bed where they collapsed onto their own sides.

Scottie waited until he was situated under the blanket then rolled into him, draping her arm over his stomach. She threw a leg over his thigh, lining their bodies up as much as she could without fully lying on top of him.

"I wish I could leave my mark on you," he said around a yawn.

She chuckled and nuzzled closer. "Maybe I'll just go get your name tattooed across my forehead."

His body shook under her head as he chuckled.

"That's a little extreme. I think across your torso would be fine."

She giggled. As her eyelids drifted closed, she focused on Jude's heartbeat, on the heavy beat of it behind his ribcage, on the way his chest rose and fell with each breath. Within moments, she could feel herself falling asleep. If she had her way, she would sleep in this exact position every night for the rest of her life. They would end every day in each other's arms after making love.

Tomorrow, everything would be different. Jude would carry her permanent mark. He would have to tell his Flock that he intended to stay with her instead of staying in the territory and figure out whether they would accept that or demand he give up his role as Alpha.

And then there were the crows. So many things were being thrown at them at once, yet all she felt as her brain began to slow and her breathing matched Jude's was complete and utter contentment.

No. What she felt was joy, true joy, the kind that only occurred when one found the person whose soul matched their own.

"Are you shitting me?" Luca asked.

"Why doesn't she stay here? We can build a place for her to work," Burke said.

Cohen simply watched everyone quietly, as did the others.

"She doesn't want to leave her house. She doesn't want to abandon her property," Jude said, rubbing a hand down his face.

"I could build a home on her property. Watch over her when you're not there," Cohen offered.

If any other male had offered to build a house on his mate's property to watch over her in Jude's absence, his animal's possessive side would have pushed forward. He might have lashed out or attacked his friend.

But Cohen only wanted the best for Scottie. He'd grown to care for her as though she were a member of the Flock, as though she were a sister.

"I don't think she wants a bunch of hawks living on her property," Jude said with a forced smile.

"Not a bunch. Just me. I'll protect her when you're not there. You live here. You stay with her at night. I'll stay there during the day."

"Even Cohen has come up with a better plan than yours," Luca said.

"I'm staying with my mate." Jude pulled his shirt collar to the side to reveal the marks she'd left on him last night.

"Damn," Burke muttered.

Luca stared at the mark.

A ghost of a smile appeared on Cohen's lips until he noticed Jude watching him. The smile fell from his face and he dropped his eyes to his boots.

"You're our Alpha. You need to stay here," Luca grumbled, crossing his arms over his chest.

"You want it? You want the title? The role?" Jude said, mimicking Luca's body language and crossing his arms.

"What?"

"Do you want Alpha?"

"Fuck no. *You're* the Alpha. This is your home. This is your Flock. *That* is your house," Luca said, jabbing a finger at the first house in the row.

Jude leaned his hip against the structure they'd built as a type of pavilion to cover their seating area.

"Either I can stay your Alpha while living with my mate or you're free to take over. Any of you. I never wanted this position. There was never a challenge for it. And there doesn't need to be a challenge for it now."

"If you walk away, the crows will see it as a weakness," Luca said.

Luca was growing angrier by the minute while Jude did everything he could to keep the peace. He would stay with his mate come hell or high water. He would never demand she completely uproot her life and try to cram all her work equipment in his single room house. It couldn't even really be called a house, for fuck's sake. It was a building with four walls and a curtain to keep any of his Flock brothers from seeing him shower or sitting on the toilet.

The way the Flock lived wasn't exactly proper or conducive for females. Especially not his mate. No way in hell would he risk any of his Flock inadvertently catching sight of Scottie while she was showering or changing her clothes.

Luca glared at his Alpha and Jude began to wonder if he wouldn't have his first fight with his Second. They'd become easy friends, had fallen into their roles without complaint, had led their Flock through the past ten years with no butting of heads.

Until now.

"Why would you automatically assume Luca would become Alpha?" one of the Flock said.

There were only eight of Skullbone Flock, with only six residing within the territory. The two brothers, Cal and Tony, kept to themselves and never balked at orders.

Which was why Jude was struck with surprise at Cal's question.

"Do you want the title?" Jude asked with narrowed eyes.

Cal silently consulted his brother before turning back to Jude. "If you're willing to walk away from the Flock for a female, maybe it *is* time for a new Alpha."

Now that pissed Jude the fuck off.

"I'm still your Alpha, asshole. You might want to watch your tongue before I rip it out."

But Cal didn't back down. Instead, he took a threatening step forward, his eyes turning silver.

Unlike predator Shifters, Flight Shifters rarely let their birds do the fighting when it came to an Alpha challenge. But Jude was more than ready to take on a challenge, not for the role as Alpha, but to keep any of his Flock from becoming power hungry.

The role of Alpha wasn't meant to lord over the others or to force his people to do things that went against their own morals. It was the Alpha's role to protect his people, to lead them, to ensure all were treated fairly and all stayed hidden from humans.

Tony reached out and grabbed Cal's arm, preventing his brother from advancing any further.

"Neither of us have any delusions of grandeur. All Cal is saying is that if you're willing to step down it should be left up to either a real challenge or, in the least, a Flock vote," Tony said.

"A vote," Cohen said with a sharp nod. "We should vote."

"If Cal wants a challenge…" Luca said with a shrug.

He did his best to appear relaxed, but Jude had known his friend long enough to see the tension in his shoulders and the excitement at the prospect of a fight in his eyes.

Cal once again stepped forward.

Well, shit. There was nothing Jude could do if the two decided they would rather a true Alpha challenge over a vote, not if he was truly willing to step down and offer up his position in the Flock.

He hated that he would have to stand here and watch as his Flock fought, hated the time he would spend away from Scottie until this was all resolved. He hadn't sent Cohen or any of the others to her house because he'd truly believed this visit would have been brief.

He couldn't have been more wrong.

Tony didn't attempt to stop his brother as he moved to an open spot of the field in front of the houses and away from the vehicles. Luca followed, a shit eating grin on his face.

Both males removed their shirts and circled each other, both waiting for the other to swing.

"If you're going to challenge, you're supposed to fight," Cohen said, mirroring Jude's own thoughts.

The longer the two danced around each other, the longer Jude would be away from his mate. And an ache had grown in the middle of his chest from the moment he'd pulled his truck away from her house and had only grown more uncomfortable in the time away from her.

Luca stopped moving when Cal stepped toward him. He bent his knees slightly and kept his arms at his side, but Jude knew he was ready to pounce the moment Cal made a move.

"You sure you want to do this?" Luca asked, that same smile on his face.

"Someone has to put a stop to the fucking crows. Neither you nor Jude have succeeded. It's time for new blood to take over."

Cal was exactly the kind of Alpha the hawks did not need. Hell, he was the kind of Alpha no group of Shifters needed. He was the type who would allow the power to go straight to his head.

Jude had never seen any of his Flock that way, had never even considered anyone he'd led through the years would see him as a failure.

"You and your brother could always move on if you don't like the way shit is run around here," Burke said. "I don't remember either of you offering up any suggestions."

At least Jude knew Burke wasn't an asshole.

"This is our Flock. This is where our loyalty has been since we joined," Cal said.

"Your loyalty? You just called your Alpha and the Second of the Flock failures," Cohen said.

The big dude didn't say much, but when he did, he sure as hell said a mouthful.

Luca turned and glanced back at Cohen.

And Cal took advantage of the momentary distraction and attacked Luca like a fucking coward.

He lunged at Luca, swinging his fist and making contact with the side of Luca's head.

But Luca didn't go down. He shook it off like a fucking champ and went straight for Cal, spearing him around the waist and taking him to the ground with a dull thud.

Tony moved forward, but Burke blocked his path. Jude couldn't foresee any of his Flock fighting dirty – although Cal *had* sucker punched the Second of the Flock – but it was better to head it off rather than wait and have to break up a brawl between all six males.

Luca punched Cal in the face once, then shoved to his feet, waiting for the other male to stand. The entire thing could have easily ended within minutes, but it appeared Luca had some aggression he needed to get out of his system. Unfortunately, Jude figured a majority of that aggression was because of *him*.

He didn't hate being the Alpha and didn't relish the idea of walking away from his role, but he would rather hand it over to any member of Skullbone instead of leaving his mate alone in her house while he stayed in his tiny cabin without her.

What he really hated, though, was watching as his Flock tore themselves apart right in front of him. But he had no right to stop them, not if he was officially giving up his title. These men were officially challenging for the head of the Flock. It was custom, even if it rarely happened.

Cal stood and wiped the back of his hand across his mouth, smearing blood along his jaw.

Fuck. They needed to finish this so he could get back to Scottie's. Whether her cat was fierce or not, he didn't want to leave her alone and unprotected any longer than necessary, especially after he'd opened his mouth and referred to her by name.

No way had Dane not noticed she meant something to Jude. And he could use that connection to bring Jude to his knees.

"I vote Luca," Cohen bellowed, stilling everyone in their tracks.

All but Luca and Cal turned to look toward Cohen.

"He's been the Second since Skullbone was formed. He knows the territory and the area better than anyone. Even better than Jude. He was born here. I vote Luca," he repeated.

"Seconded," Burke said with a grin as his hand shot in the air like a kid.

"Fuck that. I've already challenged," Cal said.

"Third…ed," Jude called out.

"Is that a word?" Burke asked, and was answered with a shrug.

As the males debated the definition of the made up word and the proper way to vote, Cal once more lunged for Luca. Luca dodged before he could take another fist to the side of the head and parried with his own swing, knocking Cal off balance for a brief moment.

"You would rather fight than listen to the people you want to lead?" Luca roared, true anger shining through his silver eyes.

Cal spit blood on the ground, once more swiping at his mouth.

It would be a fairly even fight, but Jude knew his Second would come out the victor every time. Well, except for Cohen. Jude wasn't sure whether Luca could hold his own against the big dude, not in their human form. He wasn't sure any of the hawks could best Cohen in their human forms. He was nearly as big as the bears.

"I don't like this," Cohen said.

Jude turned a frown in his direction.

"They need to finish. Scottie is alone. Too long. She's been alone too long."

"She's a predator Shifter. She'll be fine," Burke said, his attention split between Cal and Luca and Tony, making sure no one attacked while the other was unaware.

"She's a female," Cohen said.

"I'm aware," Burke said around a chuckle. "What's it going to be, boys? There are three choices: Jude stays Alpha while no longer living in the territory, we vote as a Flock, or you two continue the challenge."

"Vote," Cohen said. He moved his weight from one foot to other in obvious irritation.

"Vote," Burke said. "I vote Luca."

"Of course you do," Cal said with a sneer.

"I vote Luca," Tony said without looking at his brother.

"What the fuck, dude?" Cal nearly yelled.

"They're right – he knows the area and the people better than we do. He's been the Second for as long as Skullbone existed. We have too much shit on our plates to fight over this. You two can challenge another time."

Jude raised a brow and turned wide eyes to Luca. Tony was the last person he'd thought would be on Luca's side.

But he had a point; while the Flock was fighting among themselves, the crows were no doubt planning some bull shit to shake them up and try to get them out of the way so they could continue to wreak havoc.

Since female flight Shifters were rare, those bastards were still in the old school frame of mind that females of any species were fair game.

While they weren't as bad as the rogues who'd been trafficking women for years, they had no qualms about attempting to force a female into a pairing against her will.

Cal stomped across the field, snatching his shirt from the ground. "Fine. Whatever. When the fucker leads us into the ground, it will be on all of you."

He continued to stomp away, up the stairs and into his cabin, slamming the door behind him.

"That went well," Burke said with a smirk.

"I got to get back," Jude said.

"She's been alone too long," Cohen said again.

"Yep. Heard you the first few times," Jude said. "Thanks for the reminder."

"I can go," Cohen said.

His insistence ruffled Jude's feathers.

Turning on his heel, he stared Cohen in the eye until the male dropped his gaze to his shoes.

"Are you attracted to my mate?"

Jude had thought Cohen's apparent need to protect Scottie had been merely out of a sibling type of affection or due to a sense of loyalty to his Alpha. But the fact Cohen was offering to go in Jude's place when there was no longer any reason for Jude to stick around made him wonder if Cohen wanted Scottie for himself.

The big male's eyes shot to Jude's face. "What?"

"Are you attracted to my mate?" Jude repeated, doing his best to keep his tone level and forcing the silver from his eyes.

"No," Cohen said, his expression letting Jude know how extremely ridiculous he found Jude's question. "She's the only female in our Flock. She's my Alpha's mate. She's my sister."

Okay. So Jude had been right before when he'd assumed Cohen simply saw Scottie as a sibling, as a female in need of the protection of the hawks.

But even with the big male's words, Jude's hawk still watched closely, his wings spread and his claws extended inside Jude's head.

"I'm heading back."

"You taking your stuff?" Burke asked.

Tony shoved his hands in his pockets and made his way to his brother's cabin. He didn't bother knocking, just stepped through the door. Raised voices exploded from inside and made their way to the sensitive ears of the Shifters still standing around.

"A few. We haven't discussed the details yet. I needed to talk to the Flock first. See where I stood with y'all after moving in with Scottie."

"You sure you want to do this?" Luca asked.

He'd donned his shirt. A bruise had formed on his cheek but would be gone by morning with his accelerated healing.

"Yeah. I want to be with my mate."

No one bothered bringing up her moving to the territory again. They knew he was right, knew she and her work equipment wouldn't fit inside any of the cabins. And even if they built her a cabin specifically for her computers, that would mean she'd have to trudge there every time she had projects, including in the rain, snow, the cold. He wanted his mate comfortable. He wanted her to have everything and anything she needed to be happy.

As Jude made his way to his own house to grab a few more changes of clothing, he suppressed a groan when he noticed the steps following him across the small space and up the few stairs to his small porch.

He didn't bother making eye contact with his Second.

No. Luca was now officially his Alpha, at least after Jude officially left the territory and went to be with Scottie.

"It's not that I don't like her. She's a cool female. Brave. But..."

"But?" Jude said as he shoved clothes into a duffel bag.

"You've been Alpha since we started this Flock."

Stilling his hands, Jude took a deep breath and turned to Luca. "And I never wanted it. You know that. None of you gave me the choice. I want to be with Scottie. I want to be with my mate. If you were to stop whoring around and find a mate of your own, you'd understand."

"Then I would be tied down to one female and have to make stupid choices...like leaving my Flock behind."

Jude's nostrils flared with a deep breath. "Careful," he snarled.

99

While Jude was stepping down and stepping away, he refused to allow anyone to disrespect his mate nor his decision to spend his time and the rest of his life with her.

"If the crows make any more contact, I'll send them to you. You're in charge. But I'm a call away if you need me. I will always be a Skullbone hawk. My loyalty will always be with y'all."

Luca snorted and turned on his heel, leaving Jude's house and slamming the door behind him hard enough to rattle the few windows in the small house.

Jude hadn't realized until that moment how fucking hard it would be to walk away from Skullbone, to walk away from the role he'd held for ten years, to leave the territory.

But being with Scottie, waking up beside her every day, holding her in his arms every night, made the anger his Flock now held for him all that much easier.

Chapter Nine

Scottie leaned forward, staring at the design she'd been working on for the past two days. Her brain was fried, her eyes were tired, and, if she were honest with herself, she was having second thoughts about having Jude move in with her.

Not because she didn't want him in her home, of course. But he'd told her everything that had happened, about the almost challenge, about the anger his former Second aimed at him.

She felt responsible for all of it. Had she been more open to relocating, nothing in his life would have had to change. Instead, she'd demanded he uproot *his* life so she could have everything in hers stay the same. Such a selfish demand.

But she'd seen their homes. No way could all her furniture and her array of computers and technology fit in any of them, especially if Jude already had his stuff in there. Each of those places didn't look like they could hold more than college dorm sized appliances and maybe a small couch or love seat.

The front door opened then closed. Jude had gone to the Skullbone territory to discuss something Luca had heard from the crows, so Scottie assumed it was Cohen. He'd been the only one to come to her house every time Jude left.

She still didn't think she needed a babysitter. She wasn't stupid enough to allow someone into her house that she didn't know or trust. And she wasn't stupid enough to try to fight grown males in her human form. She would simply allow her mountain lion to burst free and rip someone to pieces if they attempted to attack her.

"Leftover pizza in the fridge," she called from her desk.

Heavy steps immediately headed for the kitchen, and Scottie smiled.

Jude always seemed slightly tense when Cohen was there, but the largest of the Flock felt more like a little brother to her. Or a bigger brother, she supposed, since he had nearly a foot over her.

Back to staring at the design, she dropped her head into her hands and rubbed at her eyes. There was something off about the mock-up but she couldn't quite pinpoint what she didn't like, and she wouldn't send anything to her client until she was positive it was nearly perfect. She had a reputation for her eye for detail, damn it.

"What's wrong?" Cohen asked from the doorway.

With a startled jump, she spun her chair to look up into his face. He'd grown more comfortable in her home, but still refused to hold eye contact for more than a few seconds at a time.

"Nothing. Stressed out over this stupid design. It's…missing something."

Cohen stepped into the room, his eyes glued to the main screen while he held a slice of pizza in one hand.

He narrowed his eyes, then leaned forward and pointed without touching the screen. "The font isn't centered."

With a frown, she turned and looked, brought up a grid, and sat up straight when she realized he was right. It was literally a hair off, imperceptible to a majority of the population, yet Cohen had caught it.

Moving it until everything was lined up perfectly, she turned off the grid and flopped back against her seat, causing it to rock.

"Holy crap, Cohen. You're awesome." That was it. That had been the problem. The font had been barely off center to the left and had changed the entire look of the graphic.

His smile was unsure at first, but then he let a grin stretch across his face and dipped his head.

"You're welcome," he said, turning and leaving her to finish up and hit save.

Satisfied with the results, she emailed a watermarked proof to the client then pushed the chair away from the desk, standing and heading to the living room.

"Any left?" she asked as she opened the fridge.

"Yeah," Cohen said around a mouthful of pizza.

She grabbed a slice from the plate and then tore a piece of paper towel from the roll as a napkin. Without bothering to heat her slice, she carried it into the living room and plopped herself down onto the cushion on the far end of the couch near the window. Cohen always sat on the end closest to the door, leaving plenty of room for her to sit without having to touch her.

"How long do you think Jude will be?"

Cohen shrugged as he chewed.

Tearing off her own bite, she looked at Cohen from the corner of her eye and wondered if she could pull information from him that Jude either refused to tell her or withheld for whatever reason. She assumed he didn't want to scare her. Or maybe he worried she would feel guilty about him leaving his territory to stay with her permanently.

"So, everyone was mad about Jude living here?"

The swallow that came from Cohen was nearly comical, like he'd forced a piece far too large down his throat.

"Not everyone," he said, glancing at her once before turning back to the show he'd been bingeing when he'd stayed while Jude was gone.

She assumed he was in the *not everyone* category but wondered if any of the others supported Jude's decision to leave the territory and willingly give up his role as Alpha of the Skullbone hawks.

"Jude said Luca is taking over for now."

Cohen nodded.

"He also said one of the guys challenged Luca but the rest of you voted for Luca."

Cohen finished his pizza, chewing slowly as though gauging his words carefully.

"Luca is fair. And he's smart. And he's been with Jude since the beginning. Cal...he's a nice guy but he doesn't think things through. He's kind of irrational at times and always wants to fight instead of looking for a better solution."

Scottie nodded as he spoke and finished her own slice.

"I'm sorry," she said after a few minutes of silence.

"For what?" he asked with a frown.

"For Jude coming here. Because I didn't want to move."

"There's not enough room. I understand. The others will, too. They just don't like change. And they don't know you yet."

Not like Cohen did. He still didn't exactly open up without her generally prompting the conversation, but he'd spent so many hours at

103

her house, they'd spent so many hours watching movies together or devouring thousands of calories while bingeing one show or another.

"They don't like me?" she asked, mildly saddened by that.

It fueled her fear of abandonment. Whether Jude had promised her he would never leave, whether he carried her mark, she still feared he would think she wasn't worth all the life changes and return to his territory and leave her in the dust.

If they were going to truly grow in their relationship, she had to learn to trust Jude. She had to learn to trust that he would keep to his word. And she had to remember not every person who came into her life would one day leave her behind.

"They don't know you," Cohen repeated.

He didn't confirm nor deny that the hawks disliked her, only repeated that they didn't *know* her.

She supposed that was the best she could ask for, for now…but she would make sure they all got to know her better. Jude had mentioned everyone getting together when it got warmer.

Thanksgiving was right around the corner. Instead of waiting for cookout weather, she would invite the Flock over to eat turkey and all the fixings as a family. She would personally make all the food from scratch in hopes of earning their favor and giving them time to get to know her. And hopefully *like* her.

But first, she and Jude really needed to set up her home to be *their* home. He'd only brought a few changes of clothing and toiletries. No furniture, no personal photos or artwork. He'd said he wouldn't drag his futon over since she had both a comfortable bed and a newish couch, but, surely, he had other stuff he wanted to bring into their shared home.

"Do you think Jude really wants to live with me?" she asked, keeping her voice soft, afraid of the answer.

Cohen had known Jude far longer than Scottie. And while she and Jude had a connection unlike any of the males had together, surely Cohen could read Jude far better than she could yet.

He stiffened and slowly turned to look at her. "Why would you ask that?"

Why the hell did he look so nervous asking?

"I'm scared he'll change his mind."

Cohen ran a hand over his short hair then dragged it down his face, scratching at the stubble that covered his jaw.

For a minute, she wondered if he would answer. Then she began to fear the answer.

But a smile twitched at the corners of his lips.

"He wants to live with you. Very much. We tried to find a way you could move to the territory, but he didn't want you to have to squeeze into his cabin or walk in the cold when you needed to work. He wants to be with you. He wants you to be happy. He likes when I'm here when he's gone because he wants you to be safe."

Wow. That was more emotion than she'd seen from Cohen in the time she'd known him. He was no longer so closed off and he'd held her gaze the entire time as though he wanted to make sure she knew he was telling the truth.

Tears burned at the backs of his eyes.

"Thank you," she said as a lump lodged in her throat.

Without a single thought, she climbed to her knees and leaned forward, hugging him around the neck.

He was tense but patted her on the back lightly until she pulled away.

"Jude will smell my scent on you," he warned.

Waving her hand in the air, she swiped a tear from under her lashes with her free hand.

"He'll get over it. If it's like you said, he needs to learn to trust me, too. And you."

They fell into a comfortable silence after that. Scottie stretched out on the couch, pulling a throw from the back and covering her legs, but being careful not to touch Cohen.

It was one thing to hug him out of gratitude. But if Jude were to walk through the door and she had her feet tucked under Cohen's thighs...she didn't want to think about how his animal *or* human side would react to such an innocent gesture.

Jude reached over and laid a hand on Scottie's thigh as they drove to Moe's. It was the first time she would have the opportunity to not only spend time with his Flock without drama, but meet a few of his friends from the Packs, Clans, and even Prides.

She'd spent entirely too much time getting ready, worried the others wouldn't like her. Why the hell she thought a second coat of that stuff on her lashes would make the hawks accept her more easily was something a male could never understand.

She was tense under his touch. Squeezing her thigh, he smiled at her when she turned to look up into his face.

"I promise it'll be fine. The Flock has calmed down. Everyone has accepted Luca as the stand in Alpha. And the rest of my friends…yeah. You'll love them. Especially the females."

Peyton flashed through his mind, and he wondered if she would be there. Scottie was nervous. Peyton's wolf might smell his mate's anxiety and burst through, ready to attack anyone and everyone she thought was a threat to Scottie.

"Are you sure you want to step down?" she asked, her brows pulled together.

"I can't be an effective Alpha without staying within the territory. And I want to be with you."

"I know. But I feel bad."

He reached for the hand that fidgeted with the hem of her shirt and twined his fingers through hers.

"There's nothing to feel bad about, Scottie. You're my mate. And my home won't fit all your…stuff. Even if we built you another place to work –"

"I know. Cohen told me about his idea. Said you two didn't want me walking in the rain and stuff when I had work to do."

A slight sense of jealousy over how close the two had grown over the time Scottie had come into their life slithered through his belly. But he pushed it away. Cohen didn't want her in that way, didn't see her romantically. He was simply treating her as he would any female who might be in the flock. Not that many hawks were born female. In fact, it was rare, the flight Shifter gene always passing from father to son.

The only female flight Shifter Jude had ever met was mated to one of the panthers in Ravenwood Pride.

He'd always wondered how many hawks had half-siblings out there who hadn't inherited the Shifter gene, whether they were aware of what their father was, if they were aware of their brothers.

"Still. You've had to leave everything behind, your home, your Flock, everything. And I've sacrificed nothing. I don't even have a mark for people to know I belong to you."

A rush of manly ego rushed through him over her words. *Belonged to him.* Of course, she didn't belong to him in the sense that he owned her. But knowing she didn't relish the fact that she didn't carry his scent in her blood like predator Shifters made him feel all warm and fuzzy.

And he realized already he was falling in love with her. Every time his heart swelled with affection for her, every time he got that squeezing in his chest, every time he worried over her safety, he was falling more and more in love with her. And he didn't give a shit that it was happening quickly.

All he knew was he wanted nothing more than to make her happy. He wanted to be the source of her joy, to make her smile and laugh as often as possible.

As well as moan and sigh as often as possible.

That was love. Wanting her happiness above his own, even if it meant abandoning his role as Alpha and packing his entire life into boxes and duffel bags to stay in her home.

Honestly, her place was far more comfortable, and not only because it was more spacious. It smelled nice and was always tidy. And she always had the best snacks in her house, although he tended to do most of the grocery shopping since he and Cohen ate way more than she did. They were both twice her size and Shifters burned more calories than humans. Shifter males burned a shit ton more.

"I like your house. And you have plenty of acreage for us both to Shift and play."

"And you still had to give up everything."

Dragging her hand to his lips, he pressed a kiss to her knuckles. "You have to put up with not just me, but Cohen on a regular basis. Two stinky men in your house...I'm pretty sure that's an even trade."

She chuckled softly. The smile stayed on her lips until he pulled his truck onto the grave lot lining the front of the bar.

"There are a lot of vehicles," she said, her eyes a little wide as her lips formed the cutest O.

"I promise it'll be fine. You'll have fun. Trust me?"

She turned and blinked rapidly. Even if he couldn't smell the fear and anxiety rolling from her in waves, it was written all over her expressive face.

"Yeah," she finally said.

Her heart fluttered like crazy at the pulse point in her neck.

Nothing he said would put her at ease. He'd learned that about her in the short time they'd been together – she needed to see for herself whether she could trust someone, whether a situation was safe, whether a person would hold to their word and not hurt her.

Pushing from his seat, he rounded the hood and pulled her door open. She stared at the front of the building a few more seconds before sliding her small hand into his and letting him help her from his tall vehicle.

A hand on the small of her back, he led her across the parking lot, weaving through the throng of cars and trucks. The soft bass from the sound system hummed through the walls and door as they grew close. As he pulled the door open, the scents of old beer and stale cigarette assailed his nose as the chatter of conversation mixed with the music coming from speakers mounted high on the walls.

"About time," a female called out over the noise.

Emory, a female from Big River Pack, smiled and waved Jude and Scottie over to where they'd scooted several tables together to fit over a dozen Shifters and their mates.

Jude wrapped his hand around Scottie's and fought the wince when she squeezed it tightly.

Emory pulled out a chair for Scottie, seating the two females beside each other while Luca sat to Jude's right.

"It is so nice to finally meet you," Emory said. "That's Nova and Gray. And the little sweetheart sitting between them is Rieka."

She then went around the table, introducing every single person from Big River Pack, Blackwater Clan, Ravenwood Pride, and Morse Pack before nodding her head toward Skullbone Flock.

"You know the birds," Emory said with a cheeky grin.

"It's, uh, nice to meet everyone."

Nova leaned forward. "We don't expect you to remember all of us by name. Except me. You should definitely remember me," she said with a wink.

As the females engaged Scottie, her hand began to relax in Jude's. The bar owner's mate, Hollyn, came over to take Jude's and Scottie's orders.

"Ohhh. Do tricks for her," Penny, a little girl from Ravenwood, said.

"Maybe later. Let's let Scottie get settled in with this crazy crowd first."

Penny looked around and nodded. "She's right. You guys are kind of crazy."

Laughter erupted. For a ten-year-old girl, Penny was funny and perceptive. And had been responsible for saving the lives of two of the mates to the panthers.

"I'll just take a beer. Uh…a Bud Light?" Scottie said.

"Got it."

"Same," Jude said.

Hollyn winked down at Scottie and returned to the bar to grab the bottles while everyone fell into easy conversation.

Until that conversation circled to the crows. Since a few of the friends of the group had brought their children, including twin toddlers from Blackwater, they used code talk the best they could and pretended to be discussing a TV show or movie.

Jude would rather not discuss any of it in front of the children. And he really didn't want to have such an open discussion about their enemy when anyone in the bar could overhear and take the information right back to Black Feather.

"Shouldn't we talk about this…in private?" Scottie whispered, leaning into Jude's side. She'd mirrored his thoughts almost exactly.

But he was no longer the Alpha. He no longer had a say in how Flock business was conducted. He could add his input, give his opinion, but in the end, it was completely up to Luca and whoever he ended up naming as his Second.

With a sigh, he shrugged, then leaned forward and pressed a kiss to the tip of her nose.

"How come he didn't bite you?" Penny asked.

All heads whipped around to stare at the little girl. She was pointing at where Scottie's shoulders were slightly exposed by her shirt.

"I thought you were supposed to bite her since you love her," the girl said to Jude.

"Penny," Ryanne, Penny's big sister and guardian, whispered in warning.

"I'm a flight Shifter. I turn into a big hawk. We don't have big sharp teeth like the wolves and bears and panthers. We don't bite our mates when we love them."

"She bit you," Penny said, turning her extended index finger to Jude's shoulder. "So, she loves you?"

Jude turned and raised his brows at Scottie. Neither of them had uttered those words. It had only been today that Jude realized he was feeling the warm tendrils of love rather than only the pull of the mating bond.

"I have big, sharp teeth." Scottie peeled back her lips and chomped her teeth together with a very human growl, causing Penny and the other little ones at the tables to giggle.

It also helped to steer the conversation away from a topic neither were comfortable addressing in front of so many curious faces.

But her hand landed gently on his thigh under the table. He gripped her fingers and turned to smile down at her. And, if he wasn't mistaken, he saw the affection he felt mirrored in her eyes.

Could she have been feeling the same as he? Could she possibly have been falling for him far deeper than simply the mating bond?

As he stared into her beautiful golden eyes, the rest of the crowd fell away. It was only the two of them. When her eyes dipped to his lips, it took every ounce of control he had not to lunge to his feet and drag her out to his truck so they could race home and make love until they collapsed into a sweaty heap of arms and legs.

Home. That might have been the first time he'd truly thought of Scottie's house as his home. He still hadn't fully settled in, hadn't fully unpacked his duffel bags into the drawers she'd cleared for him, but it was his home.

She was his home. She was everything to him. She was more than he'd ever expected to find in a mate, more than he knew he even wanted in the female his heart would claim.

And he couldn't wait to see where their life took them.

Chapter Ten

Scottie propped her chin on top of her hands she'd folded on Jude's chest. She was practically stretched out on top of him, only her legs hanging off from the thighs down.

"That…was incredible," she said through gasps for air.

They'd spent a few hours with his friends. And he was right – she'd had a blast.

The females treated her as though she'd been a part of their group for years, as though she hadn't joined them tonight. The males were nice, too. Well, there was one male who watched everyone who came in and out of the bar with intense, constantly glowing blue eyes. He'd stopped watching her closely after her short interaction with the little blonde human girl.

She'd had a great time. And the moment they'd stepped over the threshold into her house, he'd lifted her by her thighs, urged her legs around his waist, and carried her to the bedroom where he'd spent close to an hour worshipping her body and teasing her until she'd begged him for release.

Now, they laid in her bed – in *their* bed – and let their heartrates return to normal while the air from the ceiling fan cooled their dewy bodies.

"I wish I could mark you," he said as he trailed his fingertips along her shoulder.

She hummed her approval as his short nails slightly grazed her skin.

She wished the same, but it was out of their control.

"I guess you'll have to make sure I'm covered in your scent every day. However shall we accomplish such a feat?" she teased, tapping a finger against her lips as though deep in thought.

He slapped her bare ass, earning a giggle.

Rolling off his chest, she tugged the blanket up to cover her bare body, then rolled onto her side, head on her pillow, and stared at his profile.

He was so freaking handsome. He'd forgone shaving for long enough that a beard had developed, lending him even more of a rugged appeal. She'd always had a thing for men with beards. It was even better when that particular man was built like a Greek statue and made her blood boil with nothing more than a look from his icy gray eyes or a stroke of his fingers along her skin.

"How come you haven't unpacked your stuff?" she asked.

He'd told her he wasn't having second thoughts, had eased her fears that he was sacrificing far more than she was for their new relationship. Yet his stuff still sat in bags and boxes.

Jude rolled onto his side. His eyes bounced between hers until he sighed. "It feels weird."

And there went all the wonderful feelings that had been fluttering around inside her head and heart.

"Because you *are* having second thoughts," she said.

When she attempted to roll from the bed – she did not want to have this conversation completely naked – Jude grabbed her arm and pulled her back down so she had to look at him.

"I don't want to make you feel like I'm pushing myself into your life. There has been so much change over the past two weeks. And I don't mean just this," he said, gesturing to the mark she'd left on his shoulder. "I know you hate having a babysitter. I know you were used to living alone. I know you fear that I'll walk away. I guess...I just want you to be completely at ease with me and the members of my Flock before I take over your house and leave my boxers and socks laying on the floor."

She held up one finger. "One – you already leave your boxers and socks on the floor." She couldn't hide her smile. She'd teased him about putting his dirty clothes in the hamper only moments before tossing her own clothes to the floor during a heated and lust filled moment. "Two – Cohen has grown on me. He no longer feels like a babysitter or bodyguard. He doesn't bother me. His presence doesn't bother me. Actually, I forgot to tell you how he saved my sanity with one of my projects."

It had completely slipped her mind. She still didn't know what the hawks did for an income, but Cohen would be awesome with

113

computers. She made a mental note to bring it up next time he came over.

"And three – I *am* at ease with your Flock. And, even if a couple of them make me leery, *they* don't live here. *You* do. Or you're supposed to. I understand if you need time to get used to this whole situation, but you promised not to leave. And I'm trying to trust you. I'm trying to let go of that stupid thing in the back of my head that constantly warns me that you'll be like the rest of them and walk away."

"Never. I will never walk away," he vowed.

"I believe you. I really do. Or I'm trying to. But...I feel stupid saying this, but your stuff sitting packed like that makes the doubt louder."

Jude pushed up onto his elbow and looked down at her. One hand raised and his fingers pushed the hair from her face, tucking it behind one ear.

"I'm sorry. I didn't think of it like that."

His eyes roamed her face a few seconds.

"We're like one of those stupid Hallmark movies."

Scottie's brows raised to her hairline. "Huh?" Jude watched Hallmark movies?

"There's always some silly misunderstanding that causes one of the love interests to run off when the entire thing could have been cleared up with a five-minute conversation. How about from now on, if anything comes up, we discuss it instead of assuming we know exactly what the other person is thinking?"

Raising a hand, she extended her pinky. "Deal."

Looping his pinky through hers, he lowered his head until he pressed his lips to her forehead, then dropped back onto his pillow, his eyes still on her face.

"I'll never leave you, Scottie," he whispered.

He grabbed her hand and dragged it until it was cradled against his chest. And then his eyes closed. It was barely a full minute before his breathing became slow and steady.

She wished she could fall asleep that easily. Especially after opening her chest and giving him a peek inside at all the places she'd rather no one see.

But he didn't so much as bat an eye when she presented him with her deep seeded insecurities. He didn't roll his eyes or huff in exasperation when she once more voiced her fear that he, too, would leave her.

Instead, he'd done what he could to put her mind at ease, voicing his undying commitment to her.

And then Penny's little voice came to mind: Scottie did, indeed, love Jude. She wasn't sure she could say the words aloud just yet. She'd never said the words to anyone who wasn't family, and even those people hadn't stuck around.

But she would tell him. Someday. Someday soon.

Scottie wrinkled her nose and groaned at the noise coming from another part of the house. Rolling onto her back, she reached for her cell and checked the time. It was only seven thirty in the damn morning. Why the hell was Jude making so much noise so early in the morning?

She'd never been much of a morning person, and that was especially true when she was woken early after staying up so late.

Throwing the blankets off her legs, she pushed to her feet and practically stomped into the living room.

Then froze, her eyes going wide.

Several members of Skullbone were currently in her living room carrying furniture and boxes, going through Jude's things and putting them in various places...

And turning to gawk at her.

She was butt naked. In front of several males.

With a squeak of humiliation, she turned on her heel and sprinted for her bedroom, her cheeks flaming hot.

Oh shit. No no no. That did not just happen.

Tugging on sweats and a t-shirt, she dropped onto the side of the bed and put her face in her hands. No way could she face them now. It wasn't abnormal for Shifters to be naked around each other, but she wasn't nude from Shifting.

She was still naked from making love with her mate last night. Surely, they could smell Jude all over her the moment she stepped into the room.

Heavy footfalls echoed through the small space, then the front door opened and closed.

Seconds later, the bedroom door swung in and Jude appeared in the gap.

"Well then," he muttered, a crooked grin on his face.

"You could have warned me," she whisper-screamed.

"I wanted to surprise you. I forgot how much noise the guys make. I was going to get as much unpacked as I could, then make you breakfast. The guys wanted to stick around and hang out, get to know you better."

"Are they still here?" she whispered.

They were indoors but all Shifters had the same keen sense of hearing. If she talked at a normal volume, they could hear her if they paid close enough attention.

"They're waiting outside. They wanted to give you a little privacy." He didn't bother to hide his grin as his eyes raked over her now clothed body.

"I can't believe I just walked out there naked," she groaned, once more covering her face with her hands.

"Yeah. I didn't like that so much."

She peeked at him through a gap in her fingers.

Holding his hands up, Jude backtracked. "I'm not saying I'm mad you came out naked. If we were alone, I might have stopped what I was doing to take advantage of the moment. I just hate that my Flock saw my mate in all her beautiful glory."

With a sigh, Scottie dropped her hands. "They would have seen me naked eventually. I would've Shifted in front of them at some point."

She liked thinking of her life with Jude and the Flock in the future without entertaining doubts of his loyalty to her and their life together.

It took some coaxing, but Jude was finally able to convince Scottie to leave the room and face the Flock. As she'd said, they would have eventually seen her nude when she Shifted with them for one reason or another.

The Flock did their best to keep their eyes averted as they finished carrying in the things that had remained at Jude's place back in Skullbone territory. Not because they were embarrassed, but out of respect for both Scottie and their former Alpha.

And because every time any of them would glance in her direction, Scottie's cheeks would flush bright pink.

She kept moving toward the kitchen, but he would grab her by her hips and guide her away, only letting her step in long enough to pour fresh coffee into her mug.

He was still set on making her breakfast, even if it was moving toward brunch. Or even lunch.

Eventually, he got his belongings squeezed into Scottie's cabin, unpacked his clothes into the drawers she'd cleared for him, put his toiletries in the bathroom, then pulled the groceries he'd had the guys bring from the refrigerator.

"Food," he called out as he scrambled eggs, fried bacon, and pulled pieces of toast from the toaster.

The sound of heavy bodies thundering toward the kitchen made Jude smile. It had been weeks, months maybe, since the entire Flock had eaten a meal together. The only time they tended to sit and eat as a group was when it was warm enough to cook out. The air was growing colder by the day, keeping most of them inside.

"Ladies first," Cohen roared over the chatter of male voices.

Scottie appeared at Jude's elbow. "Need some help?"

"Feel free to put the plates out," he said with a wink down at her.

Her cheeks flushed that pretty pink again, but she smiled as she turned and opened a cabinet door.

Instead of carrying bowls or skillets to the table, a line formed starting with Scottie, the Flock filing behind her holding their plates.

It was definitely best for the only female in the house to go first. Male Shifters could put away some food and he wanted her to be able to get as much as she wanted before the hawks dove in.

When Jude turned off the burners and stepped back, Scottie bumped him with her shoulder and smiled. "Thank you," she whispered, although they were both aware the Flock could hear her.

She piled food onto her plate, then stepped out of the way so the hawks could get their breakfast. Or their payment, since a meal was the only thing he'd offered in return for their help in moving his things from his small house into Scottie's cabin.

"Wow," Scottie said after her first bite. "You can cook."

"How hard is it to fry bacon and scramble eggs?" Luca grumbled around a mouthful.

Scottie didn't react in any way to the male talking with his mouth full. In fact, she didn't seem anxious in any way with so many members of the Flock at her table and filling her home.

The table wasn't big enough and they'd had to pull in lawn chairs to squeeze a couple people in at the corners, but they were all together.

It was the first time he truly felt like they were all one big family instead of having Scottie in one category and the Flock in another.

He might not have been Alpha any longer, but he was still a member of Skullbone. And, now, so was his mate.

When Scottie finished eating, she pushed her plate forward and smiled as she listened to the conversation ebbing and flowing around her. It was subdued at first, but then they treated her as though she'd been with them for years.

No one watched their tongues; they busted each other's balls as they always did, and even included her in the teasing.

Eventually, the guys began to file out.

Luca jerked his head, gesturing for Jude to follow him outside. He didn't want to keep secrets from his mate, but he needed to learn what Luca had to tell him before mentioning it to Scottie.

He bent and pressed a kiss to her lips before following the new Alpha outside.

"I'll clean up when I come back in," he told her before pulling the door closed.

He probably should have had the hawks clean up after themselves, but they'd done Jude a favor. He could load the dishwasher and wash the skillets without their help.

Jude followed Luca and the other hawks to where the trucks were parked and leaned against the hood of Luca's.

"What's up?"

"I think we might have an issue," Luca said.

Jude looked over at Burke and Cohen. The brothers, Tony and Cal, hadn't offered their help, no doubt still pissed over the failed challenge.

"What's up?"

"A female from a local Pride was reported missing," Luca answered.

Narrowing his eyes, Jude pushed back the rage and fear that bubbled up in his chest.

"Anyone we know?"

Luca pushed a hand through his shaggy hair. Dude was in desperate need of a haircut.

"Eli's sister. The lion who started Hope Pride."

Jude frowned. "Emory's mate? The small female from Big River, right?"

Luca nodded.

They had hidden their fear and rage while inside Scottie's. But now that he looked around at the faces he'd known for a decade, he could see it in their eyes, in the tension in their shoulders.

"Fuck," he muttered.

"Yeah," Luca said.

"Any suspects?"

Luca simply raised one brow.

"You really think the crows had something to do with it?"

Burke rolled his neck with audible cracks of his joints. "There's always a chance we have another rogue in the area. But the groups in the area know damn well they'll be shut down if they try to Claim any females against their will."

"Killed," Cohen muttered.

"What?" Burke said, turning to the huge male.

"They won't be shut down, they'll be killed."

"Eli must be losing his fucking mind," Jude said.

"She escaped Tammen Pride after her brother took over. Managed to avoid any forced breeding. And now some sick fuck has taken her," Luca said.

Jude paced a few steps away then back.

"Are they sure she hasn't just moved or something?"

"She was taken from her home in Hope Pride territory while Eli and Emory were out with all of us last night," Burke said.

"Fuck!" Jude bellowed, the sound bouncing off the surrounding trees.

The front door opened and Scottie appeared on the porch, a frown causing a crease between her brows and a blanket wrapped around her shoulders.

"Sorry," he said to her. "It's okay."

"What's going on?"

"I'll tell you later."

Her frown deepened and she stomped down the stairs and straight to where the men were having their little meeting.

"Nope. I'm part of the Flock now, right? Since we're mates?"

Cohen huffed a laugh but dropped his head when Scottie's eyes darted to him.

Jude groaned. Burke and Luca simply stood there with raised brows.

"Yes. You're part of the Flock. But –"

"But *nothing*. What's going on that has you yelling like a fool out here?"

That got a chuckle from all the males.

"A female has been taken from Hope Pride," Luca answered.

Her brows drew down in confusion. "Those are the females who escaped forced pairings?"

"Yeah. Eli from Tammen Pride and Emory from Big River Pack started it to give the females a safe place. It was Eli's sister who was taken. Last night," Luca said.

It took a moment for the words to register. When they did, tears glimmered in Scottie's eyes.

"Last night. When we were all drinking at Moe's."

No one said anything. It wasn't a question. She was working the information through her head.

"She was taken when there were no males around to protect her." Her face went tomato red a moment before her eyes flashed a bright gold. "Fuck," she growled out.

Cohen snorted a laugh, but once again covered his smile and ducked his gaze.

"Okay. So, what do we do?"

"We?" Luca asked.

She released her hold on the blanket blocking the chill from her upper half and propped her hands on her hips. "Yes, *we*. I might not be a hawk, but I thought I was officially part of Skullbone Flock."

A hint of fear flashed through her eyes, and Jude knew it had nothing to do with the situation. It was fear of rejection. She had only just begun to believe her mate would never walk away from her, would never reject her. He told her that she, indeed, was a member of the Flock through her relationship with him.

If Luca rejected her, reminded her that she was not only not a hawk but was not technically a member of Skullbone since the two had chosen to live outside the territory, it would crush her.

Should the new Alpha declare she couldn't be a member of the Flock because she didn't live in the territory, Jude had every intention of reminding him two others had left to care for their elderly parents another county away, much further distance than Scottie and Jude.

"There is no reason to put yourself in harm's way. Yes, you are a member of the Flock as the mate of Jude, but we can take flight and search from the sky. You would have to remain on the ground. It's too dangerous."

"I have claws and teeth," she reminded Luca.

"And if we need them, you'll be the first to know. I'm sure Eli and his mate will want a part of whoever is behind this, as well. For now, we need you and every other female to stay as far from the enemy as possible."

Jude raised one brow at Luca, at his former Second in command. He was taking to the Alpha role with ease. He was doing what he thought was best for his people as well as those they had assigned

121

themselves to protect. That included any innocent female or child who was preyed upon by the sick fucks on the planet.

Crossing her arms over her chest, Scottie narrowed her eyes at Luca. "You'll let me help when it comes time?"

"Of course. We love strong women. You won't be the only female out for blood. I promise you that."

Scottie had met Peyton the night before but hadn't seen how fiercely both her human and wolf side became when her wolf believed an innocent was being endangered or exploited.

As he watched varying emotions flash through her beautiful glowing gold eyes, he realized Peyton might just have a run for her money when it came time to punishing whoever had taken Luna.

Because Scottie looked like she was struggling to keep her mountain lion from bursting forward and going after any and all suspects on her own.

Chapter Eleven

Scottie vibrated with anger. And a tinge of fear.

Although, she wasn't sure whether the fear was for herself, for Luna, or for the Flock.

If the hawks were to go after the crows alone, they could easily be overrun as they had when they'd fought over her property. Some of them could be hurt. Some of them could be killed.

And that couldn't happen. She couldn't lose Jude. She couldn't lose Cohen. And, while she might not know the rest of them as well, she had grown to care for them and was working to believe they were as committed to staying in her life as Jude was.

"You need to calm down," Jude told her for the third time since the Flock left for home.

"Has anyone ever told you that telling a female to calm down is, like, the worst thing to tell a female who's upset?"

He huffed a laugh and reached for her. She let him pull her into his arms and sighed.

"If we hadn't gone out with everyone last night, Luna wouldn't have been alone. She wouldn't have been taken."

Scottie had never met the lioness, barely remembered who Eli and Emory were, but it didn't matter. Luna was a female. And no asshole had the right to lay a finger on her. No asshole had the right to lay Claim to any female who didn't want them. The laws had been changed years ago to prevent just such a thing.

That hadn't stopped rogue Shifters from snatching females of every species – including human women – and selling them for she-didn't-want-to-know-what. Sex slavery. Forced mating. Forced breeding.

All of it was nothing short of a nightmare.

"Why does Luca think the crows have something to do with it?" she asked, pulling back to look up into his face.

His nearness was calming her rage, so she stayed in his arms, clasping her hands just above his perfectly toned butt.

A muscle jumped in his cheek. "We've been tracking the crows for a while. They're crafty mother fuckers." He shot her a sheepish look. "Sorry."

"Oh, please. You heard me say fuck outside."

Leaning down, he pressed a kiss to the tip of her nose as his body shook with a chuckle.

"They've...we don't have any concrete proof they've been involved with rogues in the past, but there are too many pieces to make anything we've found coincidental."

"But why take the lioness? Why take your friend's sister? What does Luna have to do with any of this?"

Jude had told her all about Luna, all about the incident that had occurred when Eli and Emory lived in Tammen territory, and about the development of Hope Pride after the hawks had headed home.

Luna might have avoided the atrocities of so many other females, but she'd been through far more than anyone should ever have to endure. She didn't deserve any of this.

No female deserved to be taken against their will.

A new wave of fear for the woman squeezed her heart.

"What if we don't find her?" Scottie asked, frowning up at her mate.

He pulled one arm from around her back and pushed hair from her face. "We'll find her. The guys will take turns surveilling the area and spying on the crows."

"Okay. That sounds entirely too dangerous. Even if all of you went at one time." She shook her head. "I saw how many crows were here that day. They could attack and take you guys out before you were able to tell anyone what you found."

At least Jude was there with her. At least she could sleep tonight knowing he was still in her life.

That fear of abandonment came rushing back. Death was still loss. It was the way others had left her life in the past.

She hated feeling so damn vulnerable. Yeah. Loss was a part of life. But that didn't mean she had to like it or even accept it.

"This isn't our first rodeo."

Curling her nose, she pushed away from him and dropped onto the couch, the blanket she'd worn outside still wrapped around her shoulders.

"That phrase always sounded so weird to me."

Jude chuckled and joined her on the couch but left space between them so he could turn and look into her face.

"We've been doing this a long time. We've flown over enemy territory dozens of times. We know how to stay out of sight."

"Cohen didn't," she pointed out.

"He wanted you to know he was out there. Otherwise, you never would have noticed anything out of place."

"Good point," she said, pointing her finger at him.

Leaning to the side, she rested her head on his shoulder and sighed dramatically. "Is there anything I can do to help find her?"

His cheek landed on the side of her head. "No. But I promise I'll let you know if we need back up. Luca wasn't kidding when he said there would be other females vying for blood. One of the panthers with Ravenwood Pride is mated to a human. Check this out – she hunted rogues before she ever met the panthers."

"Seriously?" Scottie said, jerking her head up and gaping at Jude.

"Yep. Kicked her mate's ass when they met. Actually, I think they said she kicked a few of their asses that first day."

Her lips stretched into a grin and she released a surprised laugh.

"That's awesome. Have I met her?"

"She was at Moe's. But there were a lot of people, a lot of names. You'll have plenty of time to get to know everyone. I promise."

There *were* a hell of a lot of people at Moe's. She remembered a few names but wasn't sure she could put them to the correct faces if she met them again.

She should probably get some work done, but after learning that a friend of Jude's had been taken, she couldn't seem to focus on anything but that, about why they weren't all in the woods surrounding the entirety of Cedar Hill and adjacent towns, and why no one appeared to be freaking out as much as she was, or at least how she was on the inside.

The last thing she wanted was for Jude to think she couldn't handle the stress. Because then he might suggest she stay behind when they looked for Luna or when they found the assholes who'd taken her and punished them. And the only punishment she felt would be enough for kidnapping an innocent female was death.

"If I'm not included in the search party, what can I do to help?" she asked.

She leaned away a bit then shoved her feet under his thighs to keep them warm. She swore she was cold from September until March. Sometimes even later when spring was late to arrive.

"There's really not much you can do. Not yet. My hope is we find her with no drama and as little blood spilled as possible. And I really hope Black Feather's Alpha is unaware."

"Because it'll turn into another war?"

"Yeah. And I know my friends will help in any way needed, but they can really only help on the ground."

"There has to be other Flocks around here. Other groups like Skullbone who would help."

He nodded, raising a hand to scratch at the stubble coating his chin. "One of the panthers is mated to an owl. Her family might help. We have two more members you haven't met, but they had to leave to care for their elderly parents. And there's a vamp in Morse Pack."

"Seriously? I've never met a vampire in real life."

She couldn't stop the excited squeal from entering her voice.

"You met her at Moe's."

Her brows dropped as she searched her memory for anyone with pale skin and pointy fangs.

Jude chuckled as he watched her and appeared to know exactly where her thoughts had gone.

"They don't look anything like the movies. They don't sparkle, they don't burst into flames in sunlight, and they're not monsters."

"Which male was a vampire?" she asked.

"Female. There's a bear in the Morse Pack. He's mated to a female vampire. Her name is Everleigh."

She snapped her fingers and pointed at Jude. "She was with that huge dude with the long hair."

126

He chuckled again, leaning to grab one of her hands so he could bring it to his lips for a quick peck to her palm. "Yeah. Zeke."

Cohen was a big male, but even *he* looked small beside Zeke. Like the rest of the bear Shifters, he was not only tall but built like a brick building.

"You're right. She looked nothing like the creatures in the movies. She was gorgeous."

Jude leaned closer and pressed his lips to hers. "Not nearly as gorgeous as you."

A breath away, she looked into his eyes. "You have to say that because I'm your mate."

He snorted a laugh as he pulled away. "Bull shit. You own a mirror."

Waving off his comment, she returned to the subject at hand before they got all mushy and gushy and rushed off to the bedroom.

Or got naked right there on the couch.

"How could the vampires help? Can they fly?"

His head wagged side to side slowly. "No. Uh. The way Everleigh tells it, various vampires have various gifts. Some can shapeshift. Others can mist or turn into some kind of fog or vapor to attack anyone at any time."

She felt her brows raise to her hairline. "Okay. Now I'm a little jealous."

Every minute he spent with Scottie, every little nuance he learned about her, made him love her all that much more. He couldn't give a shit how long they'd been together. From the moment he realized he'd found his mate, she'd held his heart and soul in her sweet little hand.

She was currently in her office finishing up yet another project for yet another client. She was never short of business and had a nice nest egg.

Unfortunately, he and a majority of his fellow Shifters weren't as lucky and had to find small jobs with Shifter owned businesses to make ends meet. Most of their homes were built themselves, but they still had electricity bills and food costs.

The latter could add up with grown male Shifters.

Jude…was currently bored out of his mind.

He'd really believed it would be easy to step down and let Luca lead. He hadn't exactly volunteered for the role nor had there been any challenges. He'd simply been assigned the title when Burke joined him and Luca in their territory and they became a Flock.

If it were a little warmer, he could go out and work on Scottie's yard. She'd told him one night when they were snuggled under the blanket that she'd always wanted a vegetable garden, and he wanted to give that to her.

But he'd have to wait a few more months.

At least Thanksgiving was coming soon. And Christmas.

The former, he got to glut himself and not feel guilty about it. The latter, he got to dote on Scottie and lavish her with gifts.

Maybe not lavish. Kind of hard to go crazy shopping when one didn't have a ton of money in their pocket. He feared she would think she had to buy him something big and fancy when he really didn't have much he could give her.

Well, shit.

His good mood was quickly turning sour. He never thought of himself as the kind of guy who would be supported by his mate. He wasn't a caveman who thought his female needed to stay home and take care of him and the house, but he never wanted to feel like he was sponging off her in any way. He was already living in her house that she paid for with her hard-earned money.

And what if they decided to have a family? It would be far too much for her to care for the baby – or bab*ies* – while still tooling away at her computers all day.

Yet, he couldn't expect her to give up a career she seemed to love to raise their pups…or chicks. They wouldn't know until the kid's first Shift.

Maybe he could ask Noah if he was hiring. The dude ran the bar and the kitchen most days. Although he did have his mate to tend bar when they were busy.

Maybe he could ask the bears if their construction company needed any help. He might fare better in a human job than the predator Shifters, but there was always a slight chance of being discovered if he let any part of his animal side peek through.

Feet propped on the coffee table, he dropped his head against the back of the couch and stared up at the ceiling, making plans to find employment. He might be getting ahead of himself, planning their future family, but he needed to do something. He'd grown so used to making the plans and barking out orders with Skullbone that he felt a little…lost.

"What are you stewing over?" Scottie asked from the hallway.

She made a beeline for the kitchen and pulled out a box of Cheez It crackers, munching on a handful as she moved closer and dropped on the couch beside Jude.

"Boredom. Lack of a concrete role."

The crinkling of the plastic bag inside the box stopped as did the munching of crackers.

Rolling his head on the cushion, he huffed a soft laugh at the look on Scottie's face.

"Still not having second thoughts, Mate. You're stuck with me for life."

The crease between her brows smoothed the tiniest bit, but she still looked unsure.

"I think I need to find a job."

The frown that appeared this time was of confusion. "I make plenty of money."

He scoffed and raised his head, sitting up so he could rest his elbows on his knees. "You happy being my sugar momma?" he teased.

"Why? Does my baby need a new watch? Maybe a new shirt?"

Yep. Every layer he unwrapped of Scottie was even better than the last. Her wit was quick, and she'd grown completely comfortable with him being in her home.

"One – feel free to buy me a new shirt anytime." Especially since he tended to go through them so quickly when he had to Shift into his hawk quickly and ripped them when his wings exploded from his back.

"Two – it's not that you don't make enough money. I've been Alpha of Skullbone for over a decade. And now…I'm just sitting on my hands while waiting to find out what we're going to do about Luna and the crows."

"*If* the crows have anything do to with her disappearance," she said, holding up her cheese coated finger.

"I don't want to sit here and stare at the walls or watch TV all day while you work your ass off to support the both of us. And what if we have a family? I don't want you to have to give up your career if you don't want, but I also don't want you to feel like you have to be the sole bread winner."

"You realize how antiquated everything you just said is, right?" she asked, her face taking on a look of both indignation and amusement.

"I'm not trying to sound old school. But I'm not much of a housekeeper –"

"I'm aware," she said, cutting him off.

"So, I wouldn't be much of a house husband."

She snorted softly when she tried to hold in her laughter.

"I'm not asking you to be a house husband. But I know how hard it is for our kind to get jobs among the humans. I also would never ask you to sit around and do nothing. I want you to be as happy as you make me. If you want to get a job, get a job. If you're content hanging around here while I work, I'd be happy to show you how to properly clean."

The last part was said with a wink.

Even if he was a world class housekeeper, he still needed something to keep his hands and mind busy.

But another issue arose when he contemplated seeking employment – what would happen if they were able to locate Luna and he was currently on the clock?

If he worked for fellow Shifters, they would understand. They might even end their work day early so they could assist in the rescue of the female and put down the assholes who'd taken her.

Hugging the box to her chest when Jude tried to grab for it, she slapped his hand away and pushed to her feet. "I'm almost done with this design. I'm in the mood for bar food. Moe's for dinner?"

He nodded. "Date night, or you want me to call the hawks?"

"Either is fine. It might be good for you to see your friends instead of only my face day in and day out."

He turned and acted like he was preparing to pounce on her. "Oh honey. Your face is the only one I want to see."

"Behave."

She grinned wide and turned on her heel, heading back to her home office where he listened to her fingers clicking on keys or the mouse as she worked her digital magic.

Snatching his phone from the coffee table, he sat back and typed out a message to Luca, telling him that Jude and Scottie planned to have dinner at Moe's later and invited the Flock to join them.

After a few minutes of thinking, he shot off a message first to Noah, then to Carter – Alpha of Blackwater Clan – asking if he knew of any Shifters hiring within thirty miles of the territory. He wanted a job, but he didn't relish the idea of being too far from Scottie all day, especially after another female had been taken.

Would Cohen be amenable with the idea of hanging out at Scottie's on a more consistent basis if Jude were to get a job?

That was yet another road he figured he could cross when he got to it. For now, there was no reason to worry about things that might or might not happen.

After a few minutes, Luca shot back a text that Skullbone would meet them there. While Jude was reading Luca's text, Carter texted that he actually had an opening in his construction crew and could use someone to man a backhoe.

Jude had literally no idea how to drive one, but he would learn. He'd bluff his way through if he had to, as long as he could bring in a paycheck so Scottie didn't have to carry the entire load of their finances.

He could still hear his mate clicking away in her office, so he decided to shower and change into something other than stained sweats and a threadbare t-shirt. Not that he had nice clothes nor really needed them. Shifters tended to congregate in rural areas and that didn't exactly require a jacket and tie.

Scottie might want to take more time to get ready, although he doubted she'd do like she had the first time they'd met up with all the local groups and don a face full of makeup or worry over her hair.

Stripping his clothes in the bedroom, he made a point of dropping them in the hamper instead of the floor, then paused in front of Scottie's office door long enough for her to get an eyeful of his junk.

"Tease," she called after him.

He chuckled, his mood lightening, as he closed the bathroom door a bit and started the spray.

Her spigots squeaked when turned. He might not be much of a housekeeper, but he could work on a little upkeep around the house.

As he stepped under the spray, he made a mental list of what tools he would need to round up to make a few repairs around the house. In general, the place was in great shape, but he wanted to be able to give her anything and everything she wanted, not just needed.

Not that she'd ever made a single comment about wanting any updates to her home.

Shit. And now he was doubting himself about making any repairs. It was her house. She should have the final say in anything done. That didn't mean he couldn't at least tighten the spigots, though.

Hair and body washed, he rinsed and yanked the curtain back and froze with his hand on the plastic and fabric.

His mate stood in the middle of the bathroom naked, every delicious inch of her skin exposed to him.

Within a half second, his dick stood at full attention and jutted toward her.

"What are you doing?" he asked, his voice husky in his own ears.

"I finished my work. I figured we could save water by showering together before heading out to eat."

"But I'm done. And you didn't step in with me," he said, his eyes roaming her body from head to toe slowly.

He would never grow tired of looking at her, would never grow tired of feeling her under his hands, would never grow tired of her wet heat squeezing his cock until he wondered if he would go insane with the need for release.

Ignoring the towel hanging on the rack, he stalked toward Scottie, unable to stop himself, and reached for her, pulling her soft body tightly against his.

They could eat later. For now, he needed to taste every inch of his female.

Chapter Twelve

Scottie paced the floor while Cohen's head appeared as though it was stuck in her cabinet.

"Nothing will materialize by staring in there," she said during her fiftieth pass from the living room to the kitchen then back.

The big male straightened and cocked one brow at Scottie.

"Neither will pacing bring Jude home any sooner."

She stopped and glared for a moment before returning to wearing a path into the hardwood floor.

"I wish they would at least call or text," she muttered.

Cohen finally settled on a box of saltine crackers. Around a mouthful of crumbs, he replied, "How are they supposed to do that when they don't currently have thumbs?"

Inhaling deeply through her nose, she blew it out in a rush, puffing her cheeks with the motion.

"I'm aware they don't currently have thumbs," she said.

The fact they were flying over Black Feather territory was exactly why she was freaking out and a huge ball of anxiety.

Not only had she seen how cruel the crows could be, Jude had told her their numbers more than tripled that of the hawks. Even if Cohen had joined the rest of Skullbone, they still would have been completely outnumbered.

Meaning they could all be easily killed. Jude had almost been killed the day they'd met. She still had no idea how the hell he'd survived crashing onto the ground in front of her porch. She would just chalk it up to fate and believe he was meant to land in her yard, she was meant to find him, she was meant to nurse him back to health and help him rediscover who he was and where he belonged.

"They're not heading into battle. I'm sure you and I both would be there if they were. They're simply going to fly close enough to gather some information, see if there is any evidence that Luna is being held by the crows."

"I highly doubt they'll have her chained up outside where anyone can find her," Scottie shot off, not caring how shitty she sounded.

"This is how we work. Stop worrying. None of us have ever been detected." He held his hand up to stop her when she pointed out she knew he was outside. "You and I both know I wanted you to know I was out there. I thought it was rude, otherwise."

The two of them had become close and he was growing more and more comfortable holding her gaze instead of darting his eyes to his feet every few seconds.

"I'm a feline Shifter. I'm stealthy. I could have snuck around the territory and used my cat's nose. It would have been easier for me to pick up Luna's scent than you guys flying overhead in hopes of spotting her."

Cohen was quiet long enough that she glanced at him during her next pass.

"What?" she asked.

"That's actually a good point."

"So, tell them."

His brows rose, his eyes widened, and he waited for her to once again remember that they didn't currently have access to their phones at the moment. She knew she would hear from Jude the second he could call her.

"Right. No thumbs," she muttered.

Giving up her pacing, she dropped onto the couch with a frustrated groan and stared up at the ceiling.

"This is taking too long." Her voice came out far whinier than she'd intended.

"It's been less than an hour, Sis. We'll bring up your idea when Jude gets back or calls."

She rolled her head and let the grin stretch across her face. "Aww. You called me Sis. You love me."

His cheeks flushed a dark pink and he averted his eyes the way he did in the beginning. She'd embarrassed him but didn't care. It was actually really sweet that he saw her as a sister, because she'd definitely grown to see him as a big brother. Regardless of the fact he was a few years younger.

"You really think it's a good idea? Me going in stealth mode to see if I can pick up her scent?"

"We'll have to visit Hope Pride so you discern hers from the crows, but yeah."

"Isn't she a lioness Shifter? I would think I could detect the scent of fur since your kind doesn't tend to carry a scent."

She wasn't sure why flight Shifters had nothing unique about their smell the way predator or furred Shifters did. She understood why they wouldn't smell of fur, but one would think they would have something extra about them that other Shifters could pick up.

"It would still be a good idea. If there happen to be other females being held there, you'll want to know for sure if Luna is among them."

Anger spiked through her system, sending adrenaline coursing like lava through her veins.

"Uh, if there are any other females being held there, we'll get them out, too. You guys wouldn't just go *oh, well they're not our responsibility*. And no way would I, either. If there are any other females being held against their will, we'll get them out and help them find their way back home."

"No shit. That's not what was I was saying. But we're looking for Luna. You need to know for sure if she's there. You don't want Eli getting his hopes up and rushing in without thinking first."

Scottie nodded and pointed at him. "Good point. You're pretty smart."

"I know."

She chuckled softly with a shake of her head as Cohen took up the other side of the couch, the box of saltines still clutched in one hand.

"Don't you at least want some peanut butter with those? Or…a glass of water?"

Before he could respond, the front door squeaked open and then slammed closed. Scottie leapt to her feet and ran to greet her mate. He wrapped his arms around her as she catapulted her body against his, and she couldn't stop the relieved sigh that escaped her lips.

"Did you find her?"

He shook his head and she could feel his chin rub against her hair with the motion. "If they have her, they have her well concealed inside the cabins on their property."

Scottie stepped back and looked into his eyes. "Why don't you let me try?" she asked, brazenly introducing the same idea she offered Cohen.

"Are you out of your mind?" Jude practically yelled. He glared at Cohen, who had joined them at a much slower pace than Scottie. "Was this your idea?"

"Uh, no. It was your mate's idea," she retorted. "I'm perfectly capable of thinking for myself. And you said I would be utilized when it came time to fight. What's the difference of me going in to see if I can track Luna in Black Feather territory?"

"The difference would be the lack of an army of Shifters at your back," Jude said through clenched teeth.

He ran a jerky hand through his already mussed hair as a muscle jumped in his cheek.

"Listen," Scottie said, taking a step closer to Jude. "You guys will be in the trees keeping watch. We can call a few of your friends for back up and keep them on standby in case someone catches my scent or hears my approach. I really think this is the best option of tracking Luna if you really think she's with the crows."

He and the rest of the hawks hadn't found any evidence that would indicate that Black Feather Crew were holding Luna captive. They wouldn't unless they were able to peek into the cabins. If they were on the ground and their senses weren't affected by the constant breeze, they might have been able to detect her scent. But so far up in the trees, it was nearly impossible.

Jude opened his mouth then shut it. Opened, then shut it again. He was trying this best to find a good argument but couldn't. He knew she was right. He knew this was the best option for finding Luna.

If she was in Black Feather territory. If she wasn't…then they were back to square one with their search.

Jude hated that his mate was right. He hated that she would slink close to the enemy's territory and all he could do was sit in a damn tree and watch from above.

He would need to bring the plan to Luca. In the end, the new Alpha had the final say. That final say *used* to be Jude's, and, as much as he wanted to pretend otherwise, it wasn't getting any easier to stand back while someone else took the reins.

If he wanted to stay in Scottie's home instead of in Skullbone territory, he would simply have to learn to accept it. She was still struggling with her insecurities about abandonment, and he would never give her any reason to think for one second he would walk away from her.

He *couldn't*. It would be no different than if someone reached into his chest and ripped his heart from his chest. It would be just as painful, and he would have as much luck surviving.

Scottie had become the other piece of his soul.

And yet, he hadn't bothered telling her what was in his heart. He'd yet to utter those three words that he'd wondered if he would ever say to a woman.

She hadn't said them, either. Jude wasn't sure whether it was because she felt as gun shy as he did, if she feared saying the words might be the catalyst that chased him away, or, his biggest fear, that she didn't quite feel the same way yet.

They had time. As long as they could make it through whatever was to come with the crows, they would have another forty or fifty years together. He could wait. He would wait as long as she needed.

"You know I'm right," Scottie said as she ran a brush through her hair.

They were meeting the Flock at Moe's. After he'd made love to his mate in the bathroom, he'd been called away for a little surveillance. It was almost eight o'clock and getting late for dinner, but he was starving and knew she had to be, as well.

He leaned against the door and watched as she pulled her hair back and wrapped a rubber band around it, securing a messy bun at the back of her head.

She didn't bother with makeup. He figured she wouldn't now that she had grown used to his Flock and no longer felt that she needed to impress them or make them like her.

Not that a lack of makeup would have made them feel one way or another about her. A majority of the females he knew rarely wore anything on their faces and preferred jeans and flannels or hoodies over fancy clothes.

"Whether you're right or not doesn't mean I have to like the plan," he answered.

She rolled her eyes and pushed past him, heading to the bedroom to slide her feet into a pair of sneakers.

Tilting her head up as she tied the laces, she said, "I'll be fine. I promise. Not like I'm going to rush into the territory and try to be Rambo."

He huffed a soft laugh and shook his head. "It's still dangerous."

"So is what you guys do. The difference is I can swallow one of the crows whole. You can't."

Jude curled his nose at the image. He hadn't thought about the fact her mountain lion might very well hunt when she ran through the woods, might kill and eat wild animals when she was deep in the forest connected to her property.

She *was* a predator Shifter. He couldn't judge her for that. Not like any of them had the choice of how they were born nor the animal that lived inside of each of them.

"Avoid swallowing any flight Shifters if you can help it," he deadpanned.

But she saw the amusement on his face and smiled.

"Eh," she said with a shrug. "They give me heartburn."

Grabbing her jacket from the closet, she tugged it on and waited for him to step out of the doorway so they could head out. The hawks would probably beat them there.

Maybe he should text one of the hawks and ask them to put in Jude's and Scottie's orders so it would be hot and ready when they got there instead of having to wait while their stomachs grumbled.

Jude pulled his keys from his pocket and twirled them around his finger.

"Why don't we ever take my car?" she asked when he opened the passenger seat and waited for her to climb into her seat.

"Because it's too small and my legs cramp."

Swinging the door shut, he rounded the hood, looking up in time to catch her watching him, and climbed into the driver's side.

A soft smile tugged up the corners of her lips when he glanced at her.

"What?" he asked as he tugged on his seatbelt.

Starting slightly, she turned her head away. "Nothing. Zoned out."

Oh, she was so not zoned out. She'd definitely been checking him out. He loved that they were still lusting after each other. Although, it *had* only been a few weeks. The fireworks didn't tend to fizzle that quickly.

Grinning like a fool, he put the truck in reverse and backed out of his space in Scottie's driveway.

He was still having a hard time thinking of it as his home, but that would come in time. And it would be way easier when he was able to financially contribute to their lives.

"I forgot to tell you – I'm going to be working with the bears from Blackwater Clan."

He saw her look at him from his periphery.

"When did that happen?"

"When you were working earlier."

"Why didn't you tell me earlier? That's awesome!"

He glanced at her and raised a brow. "Well, you were working. Then you distracted me with..." He ran his eyes over her body before turning them back to the road. "Then Luca called me to do a fly over."

"Oh. Good point," she said. "When do you start?"

"I don't know the details yet. I sent Carter a text and he said they were looking for someone to drive the Bobcat."

"I didn't know you knew how to do that."

140

"I don't. I lied. But I'll figure it out."

She laughed, then leaned her head against the rest and crossed her legs. His mate was tired. She'd worked her ass off, then exerted herself in other ways when he'd stepped out of the shower. Then, according to Cohen, had been a nervous wreck when he'd been out with the rest of the Flock.

Jude had given her the option to change their plans, had even promised to cook her dinner so she could relax. But she wasn't naïve – she knew his main objective was to avoid having to discuss her plan with Luca and the others.

Reaching across the cab, he rested his hand on her thigh, giving it a soft squeeze when she laid her hand on his. They hadn't really been able to hang out nearly as much as he would prefer. Moments like this, moments when they were alone and there was no current drama, had been fleeting for such a young relationship.

As he drove down the highway, he formed a plan in his head to give her an amazing date night as soon as they could relax for more than a few minutes. Maybe a vacation somewhere nice, or a weekend trip at some bed and breakfast type place. Females liked those places, didn't they?

The two hadn't truly discussed their futures, not really. They had each touched on the subject of having a family, but they had never decided what exactly they wanted. Well, he knew he wanted kids, but she hadn't really said whether she wanted a family. But she hadn't said she didn't, either.

Yep. They definitely needed more time alone, more quality time where they shared their dreams and all that crap.

Shit. When did he get all sappy? The last thing he'd ever thought about before meeting Scottie was getting to know someone's deepest fears and desires. But he wanted to know everything he could about Scottie.

Hand still on her thigh, Jude turned the truck into the parking lot of Moe's and cut the engine once he was parked beside a familiar vehicle.

For once, the lot wasn't packed. They would have a modicum of privacy, even if the Shifters who were inside would be able to hear every word spoken.

"Is it just us?" she asked.

He frowned at her as he pushed his door open. "The hawks are already here."

She was already climbing from her seat when he rounded the hood. He would rather her wait so he could open her door each time, but didn't expect her to change who she was for him.

"That's what I meant. Your friends aren't coming out?"

Warmth spread through his chest and made his heart swell like the freaking Grinch. *Us.* She was officially including herself in the Skullbone Flock regardless of where they lived or the fact Jude was no longer the head of the group.

"Just us," he said, a grin stretching across his face.

He didn't bother hiding it as he wrapped his hand around hers and led her to the door leading into the bar.

The hawks were situated toward the back of the bar. They'd pushed two tables together to make room and a couple of buckets of beer already sat in the middle.

"Hey, Scottie," Hollyn called from behind the bar.

"Hi," Scottie said back.

"Do you want something other than beer? They have some at the table, but I can make you something else if you want."

"Nah. Beer's fine. But I'm starving. Can I get a menu?"

Hollyn scooted them across the top instead of waiting for the couple to sit and then carrying them over.

Since the hawks were familiar – if not close – with the owner, Noah, things tended to be less formal when it came to ordering. Not that anything Noah did when it came to running his place could be considered formal by anyone's standards.

Scottie carried the menu to where the hawks sat waiting. She would be the only female at the table since they hadn't called any of their friends out. Not yet. They needed to have a concrete plan before asking for any backup.

Not that any of them would say no. The only reason any of the bears, wolves, or panthers they knew had ever sat out of a fight was because they had pups or cubs at home who needed to be watched over and protected.

142

And since the female they were looking for was the sister-in-law of a former member of Big River, he knew the wolves would be first in line to look. Well, directly behind the panthers of Ravenwood Pride. The panthers had made it their life's mission to rescue as many trafficked females while ending as many rogues as possible for the past decade.

There was no doubt they would have backup. But that didn't make Jude feel any better about Scottie being anywhere near the crows. Especially since she would be creeping close to their territory alone.

It was his job to protect his mate. How the fuck could he do that if he was perched in a tree?

"Hey," Luca said to Scottie and nodded at Jude.

Cohen pulled out the chair beside him but didn't motion for either in particular to sit.

Of course, Scottie took the seat closest to her buddy since he was the one who'd spent the most time watching over Scottie any time Jude had to leave.

With a smile, Scottie nudged Cohen with her shoulder before focusing on the small menu of limited items. Noah kept things on hand for any of the kids who came in but none of that was generally offered to the public.

"So, what's the deal?" Luca asked. "Your text was vague."

Jude lowered himself beside Scottie and scooted the chair until their outer thighs were touching.

"Scottie and Cohen came up with a plan."

"No," Scottie said without raising her eyes from the menu. "*Scottie* came up with a plan. Cohen just happened to agree."

"Okay. Then what's your plan?" Luca asked.

Setting the menu on the table, she folded her hands on top of it and laid everything out. By the time she finished, the hawks were exchanging thoughtful looks that made Jude realize they, too, thought it was a great idea.

He was definitely going to lose this argument.

"If we ask the panthers and bears to stand guard in case she needs backup, she'll be fine on the ground. With us in the trees, we'll have the air covered. No way can this go wrong," Burke offered.

"You saying those words alone makes me all the more apprehensive about all this shit," Jude said.

"You know she's right. And I'm right," Burke said.

Jude's nostrils flared as he inhaled deeply and blew it out in a rush. They were both right.

Didn't mean he had to like any of it.

If it were up to him, she would stay somewhere safe while he and the hawks figured it all out. Even if there was a battle, he would rather she not be involved. There were far too many ways she could get hurt or even killed.

Instead, he would have to watch from above while his mate slunk close to Skullbone's enemy and pray she was able to remain as stealthy as she claimed.

Chapter Thirteen

"We got you girl," the human, Campbell, said.

After seeing her face to face again, Scottie remembered her. And, according to Jude, she was the woman he'd told her about who'd hunted rogue Shifters long before becoming mated to one of the panthers.

It was an oddly romantic story.

The way Jude told it, Campbell kicked Brax's ass when he tracked her, thinking she was a victim. And he fell instantly in love.

Any other time, Scottie would think it was unwise and downright ludicrous to bring a human woman into a situation like the one they were planning. But if she'd been able to defeat so many rogue Shifters on her own, there was no reason to think she wouldn't be helpful in a fight.

There were currently twelve predator Shifters and eight flight Shifters congregating in her driveway, including Eli, Luna's brother, as they solidified their plans, decided who would stalk closer with Scottie and who would linger downwind and wait for word that they were needed. *If* they were needed.

She seriously hoped they weren't needed.

A fight wasn't exactly something she had ever shied from, but if these people rushed in to protect her, they could end up getting hurt or worse while trying to keep her safe.

She had to remember why they were all there. She had to remember there was a female who was possibly being held by the crows for unknown reasons.

Jude stayed within touching distance the entire time, his hand grazing her lower back, stroking along the back of her arm, or resting on her shoulder. It was as though he was afraid to refrain from touching her for fear she would disappear.

"I say the bears follow while the others linger downwind," Luke from Blackwater said.

"No. I think the female wolves would be lighter and would make a lot less noise," Emory, Eli's mate, replied.

Several of the males frowned and shook their heads, including Eli. "I'm going," he said.

"I know we don't know each other well," Scottie said, tamping down her anxiety when all eyes turned to her, "but I really think it's a better idea if you hang back. I know if someone I loved," she said with a glance in Jude's direction, "was being held against their will I wouldn't be able to control myself. We don't need to start a war without knowing all the facts. We don't know how many crows are there. We don't even know if Luna is in Black Feather territory. I think Emory's right. The females are lighter and will make less noise. And, since you big, strong boys will be close behind, you can rush in if we happen to be heard or detected and need some back up."

The females grinned. A few raised a fist in triumph, including Campbell.

"You're staying back with us," her mate, Brax, said.

Reaching up, Campbell patted his cheek. "After all this time and you still think I follow orders."

He shook his head but couldn't hide his smile. It was obvious he would lose any further argument if he tried to demand she linger back with the males.

"So, when do we do this?" Peyton, a blonde with purple streaks asked.

She was the female who'd started out human and had her wolf forced into her and had nearly died during her first Shift. Since then, her animal was a little unhinged and tried to attack anyone or anything who she deemed a threat to…well, anyone she cared for or saw as vulnerable.

There were wolves, lionesses, a cougar, a human, an owl, and even a vampire. They might all have been females, but they were definitely a collection of warriors. And she was glad they were on her side.

After at least an hour of arguing and plotting and planning, they decided on their exact course of action. They would park their vehicles in an abandoned property, walk deep into the woods, then everyone but Campbell would Shift. The hawks and Marisol the owl would head out first, circling wide to remain out of sight and land high in the trees surrounding the area.

Since they couldn't exactly signal to each other, the females would try to time it to when the hawks were ready for them to move forward. The females at Scottie's back would stay hidden twenty yards behind while Scottie continued to sneak forward.

Any of the predator Shifters could have done exactly what she had volunteered for, but it was her plan and she wouldn't allow anyone else to risk their safety in her place.

The males would hang back another twenty yards, putting forty yards between them and where Scottie planned to hide and do some surveillance of her own.

Her heart raced as she climbed into Jude's truck. His hand landed on her thigh and squeezed a little tightly, his fingers digging into her leg through her jeans. Apparently, he was as nervous as she was. Although she knew it was all about her safety and not his own.

"It'll be fine," she said, gripping his hand and turning a forced smile at her mate.

She was trying to reassure Jude but repeated the words in her own head to confirm to herself that there were more than enough people to watch over her should the crows notice her presence.

"You have to come back to me," he said. His voice was thick like he was choking on emotion.

"I promise. I'll always come back to you."

He pulled the truck in behind the other vehicles and killed the engine. Pulling off his seatbelt, he turned and cupped her face in both hands.

"I love you, Scottie. I've wanted to tell you that but…whatever. It doesn't matter. I just need you to know how much I love you. How deeply in love with you I am."

Tears pricked the backs of her eyes. She blinked rapidly to keep them from falling over her lashes. With a watery smile, she pressed her hands to his, keeping them in place, and said, "I love you, too, Jude. I'm pretty sure I fell in love with you the moment I heard your voice."

He didn't smile. He didn't speak. He leaned forward and pressed his lips to hers, not deepening the kiss but simply breathing her in, soaking up everything he could.

"When this is over and we're behind closed doors, I intend to remove every piece of your clothing, kiss every inch of your body, and make love to you until neither of us can move. Then, we're going to sleep for at least two days."

Her smile spread as she nodded. "Sounds perfect."

They stayed exactly the way they were for several more minutes until someone slapped the hood of the truck.

With a sigh, she pulled away and undid her seatbelt with shaking hands. She didn't want Jude to know how scared she was, to see how nervous this whole plan made her. She knew he would put a stop it and they would be no closer to finding Luna.

Actually, she had a feeling if she didn't head out soon, Eli might very well rush headfirst into Black Feather territory and start bursting through doors and windows in search of his sister.

They had to do this as quickly and quietly as possible. It was best to avoid a battle if it could be avoided. Lives were often lost any time Shifter groups battled and she refused to lose any of these people, even those she was only just getting to know. She wanted them in her life. Like Jude, they were the loyal type and she actually trusted they wouldn't walk out of her life without a backward glance.

For the first time in her life, she felt as though she had people who wanted her there, people who cared for her regardless of how long they had all been in each other's lives. She felt as though she was growing this big, crazy, beautifully dysfunctional family and couldn't wait to see what the future held for them all.

They just had to get through the next couple hours.

"You ready?" Emory asked.

The female wolf was a couple inches shorter than Scottie but there was something about her, a fire in her eyes, that let Scottie know Emory would be a fierce fighter if it came to that.

In fact, every female there looked as though they were ready to charge forward and kick some ass.

Once the entire group was far enough in the woods, they all began to remove their clothing and left them folded or crumpled in piles on the dried leaves and twigs.

The males kissed their mates.

The flight Shifters burst into the sky with nothing more than the sound of their wings flapping in the wind.

Then the predator Shifters all dropped to their hands and knees and let their beasts take over. As one huge line of fur, teeth, and claws, they crept forward, barely rustling the foliage around them.

The males halted while the females continued forward.

And then it was only Scottie moving forward.

Her mountain lion had zero apprehension about the job at hand, but Scottie watched through her animal's eyes and prayed their stealth would keep them hidden from Skullbone's enemy.

Lowering until her belly nearly touched the ground, Scottie's mountain lion crept forward until she could clearly see, hear, and smell everything in Black Feather. No one was out and about in the dark, but several of the small cabins, trailers, and tiny homes were lit from the inside.

She smelled wood smoke, food cooking, even what she assumed was laundry detergent or fabric softener. But no fur blew on the breeze. She was downwind so the crows wouldn't smell her, but if there were any predator Shifter females being held in the territory Scottie would be able to smell their fur.

Nothing. Nothing out of the ordinary.

Luna wasn't there.

Well, shit.

This wasn't the news she wanted to take back to Eli. Not that she wanted Luna held by anyone, but if she was in Black Feather, at least they would be able to liberate her safely and get her home.

Instead of returning to where the females waited, Scottie's mountain lion took it upon herself to creep forward even closer while Scottie screamed in her head to stop, to turn back, to run back to Jude.

Her cat's paws were silent as they padded along the ground, bringing her closer and closer until she was right beside the first cabin in the row.

Leaves rustled overhead. A few still clinging to their branches fluttered to the ground right in front of Scottie's lion.

Jude. Or one of the hawks. They were warning her to stop, warning her that she was taking too much of a risk.

Yet Scottie couldn't convince her animal to turn back. It was like screaming into a void for the good her demands were doing.

Raising her head into the air, Scottie's cat inhaled deeply, dragging every scent surrounding her deep into her lungs. Still no fur, nothing that would indicate either human or Shifter females were being held against their will.

A door opened and slammed shut. Feet thumped down the wooden steps outside one of the homes. And then those feet crunched across gravel and dried leaves in her direction.

Unlike the panthers, her fur wouldn't blend into the night. Lowering all the way to her belly, Scottie's cat watched, listened, and waited to see if the crow male would spot her, if he would notice her tawny fur against the dark woods at her back.

Shit. This wasn't good. If he spotted her, she knew he would sound the alarm. Which, in turn, would bring all those in the trees and in the woods rushing to her side. She didn't want to be the one to start a fight but couldn't convince her animal to retreat.

There was no fear in her beast's head or heart. There was something else, something Scottie couldn't identify, something akin to curiosity and confusion.

What the hell was there to be confused about? The crows obviously hadn't been the ones who'd taken Luna, or at least they weren't holding her in their territory if they had been behind her abduction.

Perhaps that was the reason her lion was lingering; she was hoping to find evidence one way or the other that Black Feather had been behind Luna's disappearance. She continued to sniff the air, searching for any scents of fur, blood...fear.

At least there were no lingering hints of blood on the air. That had to be a good sign that Luna was still alive, right?

Or, it simply meant the crows had nothing to do with her current state and they were looking in the wrong place.

The male who'd stepped outside lit a cigarette and puffed on it a few times. After a few minutes, he dropped it on the ground and snuffed it out with the toe of his shoe before returning to his home.

As soon as Scottie's cat was alone, she began to slink backward, her belly still low, until she was far enough to avoid her scent being picked up by anyone else who might step outside.

She then turned and jogged toward where the females waited for her, their ears back, their eyes glowing with rage and fear, their bodies poised and ready for action.

As a group, they turned and jogged through the dark woods, their only light coming from the moon dappling the ground through the bare limbs overhead.

Scottie knew Eli would be disappointed. She also knew her mate would be angry that she'd taken the risk of moving entirely too close. But, to her defense, she'd simply been along for the ride while her mountain lion had taken full control of their actions. All she could do was pray that she wouldn't be found.

And that Jude wouldn't be too enraged.

Jude had nearly worn a bare patch into the ground as he paced back and forth, waiting for Scottie and the other females to join them where they'd all left their clothing.

The hawks and Marisol were currently dressed and waiting. The males circled the females, flanking them on all sides with Campbell walking beside her mate, her fingers stroking down his fur.

He had no idea how Brax didn't lose his mind every time Campbell went into danger, how he didn't lose his shit every time she came up against a Shifter male.

But he also knew enough about Scottie to know the two would butt heads in a serious way if he ever attempted to dictate any part of her life.

Evidenced by the fact she'd fully entered Black Feather territory completely alone.

The females covered their breasts and lower halves while the males cupped their junk in their hands. It wasn't uncommon for Shifters to be nude around each other, but it also wasn't wise for so many naked females to be around so many mated males. Just because their human sides knew no one was ogling their mate didn't mean their animals wouldn't behave in a more primal manner and attack.

The moment Scottie came into view, Jude rushed forward, sweeping her into his arms and crushing her against his body. Yeah. He'd been able to watch her from above. But he needed to feel her against him, to feel her in his arms, to know without a doubt he was unscathed and safe.

When she grunted, he realized he might be holding her too tightly. Releasing her, he grabbed her by her shoulders, bent his knees until they were eye to eye and frowned. "What the hell were you thinking?"

"Uh, not me. My cat was determined to get as close as possible."

"You didn't tell me she was unstable."

Scottie mirrored his frown. "Excuse me, she is not unstable. She was determined to find Luna."

"Nothing?" Eli asked.

Both Jude and Scottie turned toward him. His face was a mask of utter and complete agony and rage.

Scottie shook her head while Jude blocked her bare body with his own. She bumped into his back and when he glanced back, she was tugging her shirt over her head.

Stepping around him, she twined her fingers through his and looked from face to face.

"Nothing. I smelled nothing out of the ordinary. And my cat was intent on getting as close as possible. I didn't smell any fur, didn't hear anything that would make me think anyone was being held against their will in the crow's territory." She gave Eli a look full of pity. "I'm so sorry. I really hoped she was there so we could go in, kick some ass, and bring her home."

Eli nodded and turned on his heel, walking away a few steps before tilting his head back and bellowing, "Fuck!"

Emory rushed to his side and wrapped her arms around his waist, whispering words that were meant only for his ears.

They were still close enough to Black Feather's territory that they could be heard, at least if Eli continued to roar his rage.

Scottie watched the duo for a few seconds before speaking up again. "We'll find her, Eli. There are enough of us. We can keep looking. I personally volunteer to look anywhere and everywhere. And the hawks will continue to search from the sky," she said, tilting her head back to look into Jude's face for confirmation.

He nodded. "We won't give up, dude. We'll take turns scouring from the sky until we find something."

"We'll look from the ground. We'll call in some friends if we have to," Carter from Blackwater said.

As the moon lit on Eli's face, tears glistened in his eyes. But he nodded as though he was unable to get any words past his throat.

Once everyone was dressed, they stalked through the woods to where their vehicles were parked.

"It's not too late yet. Why don't we go grab a beer at Moe's?" Scottie offered.

Jude looked down at her as his brows raised to his hairline. The first time he'd taken her to meet a group of his friends, she'd been a nervous wreck. But in the weeks since they'd met and become mates, she'd grown comfortable around not just the hawks but many members of the various Packs, Prides, and Clans who'd become a family.

Jude checked the time on his phone. Moe's would be open for at least another hour. If they left now, they would have at least thirty or so minutes to relax with a beer.

"Not tonight," Eli said. He didn't bother forcing a smile or even pretending he was okay.

Jude couldn't imagine how he felt. Luna was his younger sister as well as a member of the Pride he'd built for the females who'd escaped forced Claiming and asshole mates. Without saying a word, it was obvious Eli blamed himself for failing his sister, for not protecting her, for leaving Luna and the other females alone while he went out with his friends.

How the hell could he have known something like that would happen? It'd been fairly quiet for a while. Almost too quiet for so many Shifters who'd grown accustomed to constant action and assholes who treated females of every species like they were no better than cattle or some other livestock to be bred for their own gain.

Fuck. They had to find Luna before any damage was done to her body or mind. They had to find her before Eli lost his damn mind and tore the entirety of Cedar Hill apart in search of her.

They had to find her before it was too late, before she was lost to Eli and her friends forever.

Chapter Fourteen

Scottie stood on the front porch, a blanket wrapped around her shoulders, a mug of coffee gripped in both hands. It was a cold morning, but she needed some air and some space to think.

She had really hoped Luna had been there last night, had hoped to bring her brother good news, had hoped to get her home.

Instead, she'd brought nothing but more misery to the poor guy.

She knew it wasn't her fault, but that did nothing to make her feel any better about the situation.

There really had to be more they could do than the hawks flying around overhead while the ground Shifters checked various areas. Not like they could call in the human police for help. But why couldn't they do some form of a search party?

Because it would bring way too much attention to the Shifters. The easiest, fastest, and best way to search for Luna would be in their animal forms. Their sense of smell was far more acute as beasts, and they could move faster and fight far better when they had fangs and claws.

As she sipped on her coffee, she ran the night before through her head. And then Everleigh's face came to mind.

Pushing through the front door fast enough that she splashed the scalding liquid over her hand, she set her mug on the counter as she passed and jogged down the hall to where Jude still slept.

"Hey," she whispered, touching him on the shoulder.

It took a few tries, but finally, his lids lifted and he blinked drowsily up at her. "Morning," he croaked out.

"You said the vampires have different abilities, right?"

His dark brows drew together. Raising his hands, he scrubbed the heels against his eyes.

"Yeah?"

"So, can't they help find Luna? You said they had skills like misting or whatever. Do any of them have, like, telepathy? Or can they turn into bats and skim an area without anyone noticing them?"

Jude scooted until his back was against her wooden headboard and gave her a thoughtful look. His eyes darted to the side then back to her.

"I'll have to call Zeke, see if he can talk to Everleigh. From what I understand, the vamps don't have much to do with other Shifters. They see all of us as inferior."

"That's kind of crappy," Scottie said.

He lifted one shoulder in a half shrug. "Is what it is. I've only heard rumors of the various abilities and gifts. I'll have to find out if they have any that could help track down Luna or the person who took her. But that's a pretty damn good idea."

"Thanks. I'm full of them lately."

"You're full of something," he muttered, and swatted her ass as she crawled off the side of the bed. "You working today?"

"I just need to finish up a small project. Call Zeke. And the hawks. And whoever else. Let's have a powwow and figure this out. I hate thinking about that poor female out there waiting for someone to save her. She must be terrified."

He scrubbed both hands down his face and threw his legs over the side. "I'll make the calls. Is there coffee?"

"Yep. I couldn't sleep. Woke up before the rooster."

He frowned. "You don't have a rooster."

Sucking her lips into her mouth, she tried to hide her smile and failed miserably. A bark of laughter escaped.

"You're not fully witted when you wake up, are you?"

He gave her a sleepy smile and a shake of the head a moment before she stepped out of the room and into her office.

Then stepped back out when she remembered her coffee was still sitting on the counter getting cold.

"Damn it," she muttered when she took a sip.

She wasn't opposed to iced coffee but wasn't a fan of lukewarm coffee.

Topping it off with some fresh brew, she hurried back to her home office to finish up the work she had planned for the day. She could always work on more, but she wanted to keep the day light so she could join Jude and the others in their quest.

Scottie chuckled to herself. She'd seriously just turned the day into some fantasy movie or something, like they were in search of some magical creature who could help solve their problem.

But wasn't their entire life one big fantasy? Their kind wasn't supposed to exist in the world and were written about by humans, although they rarely got the facts straight.

And Jude was currently contacting a real-life vampire in hopes she and her kind could help them find a damsel in distress and get her back to safety.

Her hopes were rising again. She just prayed this time they wouldn't be smashed to bits the way they had been last night.

Poor Luna. Scottie didn't even want to think about what the poor woman was going through. She wasn't sure she could survive something like that. Not mentally, anyway.

As she typed and clicked away on her mouse, she could hear Jude's rumbling voice carry through the house. She did her best to tune him out and focus on her work, but periodically, she'd catch a few keys words. It sounded like he was arguing with someone.

Hopefully, whoever he was arguing with would see reason.

Within thirty minutes, she finished the small task she'd assigned to herself for the day and hit save. Sending it to her client for the first round of approval or edits, she rolled her chair back, swiveled, and planted her feet on the ground in one smooth and fluid motion.

Jude was pacing the living room, the phone pressed to his ear, his free hand rubbing his forehead and temples as he listened to the person on the other line. Straining her ears, she tried to listen in without moving closer and being super obvious. All she could hear was the deep rumbling of a male voice.

Whether or not the vampires decided to help, she made up her mind that she would head out on her own to do a search if she had to. Every day Luna was missing was another day she could have been suffering one atrocity after another. Scottie might not have been able to take on a group of Shifter males alone, in crow *or* human form, but if she could just pinpoint Luna's location, she could call in the cavalry and get the female the hell out of there and back to safety.

She was still wearing a pair of lounge pants and a sweatshirt, so the first thing she did was change into a pair of older jeans and grabbed her shoes and socks. She never wore her nicer clothes if there was a possibility she would have to Shift quickly and destroy whatever she was wearing.

Jude had stepped outside and was pacing the length of her covered porch as Scottie sat on the couch and donned her shoes. She twisted her hair back into a loose bun at the back of her neck and wrapped an elastic around it, securing it enough so it wouldn't get in her way if she had to traipse through the woods in her human form.

One way or another, they were getting Luna back as soon as possible. Preferably today.

Nerves burned her stomach, but she refused to entertain the thought of changing her mind. The nerves and fear Scottie was experiencing were nothing compared to what Luna could have been experiencing.

And Luna wasn't the only person suffering. The look of pure agony in Eli's eyes last night had nearly shattered her heart.

There were other people who loved Luna, as well. There were other females in her Pride as well as Emory who wanted their friend and sister back.

Yep. Scottie would do what she had to to ensure the female was returned to her normal life but seriously prayed she would have help.

Okay, yeah. She knew Jude and the hawks would help. Knew his friends from the other Packs, Clans, and Prides would help. But at the moment, they had no idea where Luna was being held, had no idea who had taken the lioness.

That was why they needed the vampires. And maybe some other flight Shifters. The mate of one of the panthers was an owl. Surely, her family would be willing to help if it meant saving an innocent female from some asshole.

By the time Jude stepped back inside, she was fully dressed with a heavy jacket draped over the back of the couch in anticipation.

"Well?" she asked.

His sigh and the look on his face was full of exasperation.

158

"Eli is about to lose his shit. The lionesses in Hope Pride are up in arms and terrified to be left in their territory alone. Gray and the rest of Big River are struggling to keep Eli from running off half-cocked after the crows."

"Damn," she muttered. Eli was a big guy and a lion Shifter. She couldn't imagine what it would take to keep an unhinged Shifter his size in check. "What about the vamps? Or some more flight Shifters?"

"Mason's mate is going to ask her family Parliament to see if they would be willing to help. Zeke said Everleigh is already in discussion with her family Coven to see if any of their members are able to help."

"So…we're back to waiting," Scottie said.

His eyes scanned her from head to toe. "Are you leaving?"

"I'd hoped we had something to go on and could head out as soon as you were off the phone."

Jude lowered beside her, dropping heavily like his legs no longer wanted to hold him up.

"You look tired," she said, running her hand up and down his back.

"I am now."

He scrubbed both hands down his face then dropped back against the cushions. "I don't know why I thought that would be an easy call."

"Nothing about this is easy. I can't even begin to imagine how Eli feels. Or the lionesses in Hope Pride."

It didn't surprise her that they would be afraid of being alone after one of their members was taken from her own damn house. Luna should have been safe in her own home in her own territory. No one should have to fear being alone locked inside what should be their sanctuary and haven.

"If the crows don't have her…" She leaned her head on his shoulder, then shifted against his side when he lifted his arm. "Does Eli have any enemies? Are there any other groups of rogues hunting the area for females?"

"There's no way of telling whether there are other rogues in the area. Ravenwood has been hunting those assholes for over a decade. But there will always be one asshole or another whose moral compass is fucked up. And I have no idea whether Eli has any enemies. Although

159

I'm sure there are still some jackasses in Tammen who are pissed about their Alpha being taken out then Eli walking away."

She tilted her head back to look into his face. "Eli was with Tammen?"

"Yeah. He marked Emory when Tammen attacked Big River."

Scottie sat straight up. "Eli Claimed Emory against her will?"

He didn't come off as the kind of jerk who would treat a female like that.

"It's not what you think. He apparently knew she was his mate and marked her to protect her from his own Pride. When Tammen's Alpha was killed in the fight, he took over as Alpha. The rest is a long story and not mine to tell. But after he walked away from his Pride, he and Emory developed Hope Pride so the females who escaped had a safe haven."

Okay. That was a little less dickhead-ish than the way he'd originally stated it. At least it had worked out well. Emory and Eli appeared to be crazy about each other and truly, deeply in love.

"Maybe we should go to Hope. Or Big River. Maybe if Eli's surrounded by friends, he'll remain...I don't know, calm. Or at least there will be plenty of people to restrain him if he tries to rush off."

He dipped his head and kissed the tip of her nose. "Are you done working?"

"Yep," she said.

"It's not a bad idea. If nothing else, we can offer him support. And we'll be together if we get some backup for the search party."

"See? Full of good ideas."

As she snuggled into his side a few more minutes, she couldn't help but be amazed at how far she had come emotionally in the short time since Jude had crashed into her life. She'd gone from being terrified of commitment for fear of abandonment to embracing all these new people and trusting that their loyalty was real.

There was still a chance they could have been taken from her during battle or even with old age. But she had to remember death wasn't the same as abandonment. Neither Jude nor any of the new people in her life would ever walk away from her voluntarily.

160

In such a short time, she'd found a mate, a group of friends who were quickly feeling like family, and had developed what she felt was a huge amount of emotional stability and maturity.

But she'd feel a hell of a lot more stable and content once they found Luna, punished the asshole who'd taken her, and got back to their normal lives.

It was way too chilly to have a get together outside, but none of the houses in any of the groups would hold the number of Shifters who now sat around the fire pit in Big River territory. The only people missing were the toddlers. There were a couple of younger girls, one of them human, who ran and played with a huge Rottweiler that belonged to Campbell. But the younger cubs and pups were hanging out with a couple of females inside the Alpha's cabin with their mommas.

Eli sat forward, his elbows resting on his knees, his focus solely on the fire that crackled and popped. The male looked as though his lion was on the edge, as though Eli's human side was struggling to maintain his flesh, as though Eli was struggling to keep his lion from bursting free and running off on a murder spree.

His mate, Emory, sat beside him, her hand making slow paths up and down his back. Even she looked as though she were struggling to keep her wits about her.

Big River's Second, Micah, and Tristan's mate, Peyton, were no better. Their eyes glowed bright blue and neither could sit still, sitting forward then leaning back.

If something didn't happen soon, Jude worried the group would erupt into an explosion of fur and feathers.

The door to the Alpha's house opened and Nova stepped onto the porch, a huge cooler in her hands. "Someone come get this. Every one of you look like you need booze."

The big bear Shifter, Colton, lunged to his feet and jogged to the porch, taking the cooler from Nova.

He carried it to where the group sat and set it near the center while keeping it away from the heat of the flames. Without asking, he started pulling bottles from inside and handing them over. Each person passed it on to the next until every single Shifter in the huge circle had a beer.

Eli didn't bothered popping the top off his, simply gripped it between his hands.

"You're going to break the glass," Emory muttered to him, prying the beer from his hands and setting it on the ground near his feet.

If Eli heard her or noticed he no longer held the bottle, he didn't react in any way, only continued to stare into the dancing orange and yellow flames licking at the stack of wood.

A phone chirped from somewhere down the line. The big bear Shifter who resided with the Morse Pack leaned forward and pulled his phone from his back pocket.

"It's for you," he said, handing it to Everleigh.

"Hello?" she said. "Hey, Dad."

Everyone tensed; their eyes turned toward her as they all waited. Everleigh barely said more than two words the entire conversation. She listened and then finally turned a smile on Zeke.

"You're amazing, Dad. Thank you so much."

Ending the call, she handed the phone back to Zeke, then looked at Eli. "A member of my family Coven found her."

Eli lunged to his feet, his body vibrating with the need to Shift. "Where?"

"About an hour from here. She's being held by a hyena. A crow was spotted coming and going, but only the one."

"So, the crows are involved?" Scottie asked.

Jude wrapped a hand around hers and squeezed.

"The Coven member didn't see any others and she was never moved from a hunting cabin that had been abandoned by humans long enough ago that the building is being held together by a group of termites holding hands."

Jude assumed she was attempting to make a joke, but the air was filled with so much tension no one so much as cracked a smile.

Everleigh cleared her throat and turned her attention to Eli. "My father is offering the force of the Coven if needed."

"My family Parliament is willing to help, as well," Marisol spoke up softly.

"You know we're in," Aron, the Alpha of Ravenwood said.

"The bears are in," Carter said.

"Hell yeah," Reed from Big River said. "It's been way too long since I was in a good brawl."

"Language," his mate, Lola, said from beside him, nodding toward the little girls who'd stopped running with the dog and were now watching their parents and surrogate aunts and uncles closely.

Even the little human girls appeared to sense the gravity of the situation without anyone mentioning details around the children.

"Don't say hell, Gracey baby," Reed said, turning in his chair to look back at his daughter.

"I know, Daddy."

"Where are we heading?" Gray asked.

While Eli and Emory might have led Hope Pride, they'd built their territory inside of Big River's territory. It was extra protection for the damaged and easily spooked females who arrived there in search of solace and safety.

Words weren't needed to know Gray and the other members of Big River felt as responsible for the lionesses as Eli and Emory. They felt equally guilty for Luna's disappearance.

But because Scottie had the idea of reaching out and extending their resources, they now had a lead on where to find Luna. They had backup by several groups if needed.

Luna would be returned to her family and friends by the end of the day.

All Jude could do was pray that none of his people or friends were hurt or killed in the process.

Chapter Fifteen

Scottie had been waiting for this moment, had planned for it since she'd sipped her coffee and wondered if the vampires would help.

Lie. She'd been ready for this moment since she'd heard of Luna's abduction. She'd been ready for this moment since the hawks had taken flight and tried to scan Black Feather's territory. She'd been ready for this moment since her mountain lion had slunk into the crow's land in search for any hint of the female's presence.

Yep. She was ready. But that did nothing for the nerves that turned her stomach and sent adrenaline burning through her veins.

Groups had broken off and were making plans, wishing each other luck, and kissing their children and the mates who would remain behind goodbye to pleas of a safe return.

She hated there was a chance someone might not see their mate again. Hated that one of these people might not see their pup or cub again.

That wasn't an option. She never wanted to say goodbye to Jude, but she would gladly put herself between any of them and certain death, especially if it meant a child wouldn't grow up without both their parents.

Not that she had any desire to die at an early age. And she sure as hell didn't want to live a life without Jude, yet she was prepared to sacrifice herself for someone else.

This whole thing was twisting her up inside. All those old fears of abandonment threatened to rear their ugly head, but she refused to acknowledge them. No matter the outcome tonight, she knew Jude would never leave her willingly. Should his life be ended, she knew it would be because he was honorable and protective of those he loved and cared for, not because he didn't want to live to a ripe old age with Scottie by his side.

She had to push all those thoughts out of her head and focus on the next step. They had a location for Luna, they knew the run-down cabin

164

was being guarded by hyenas, of all things, and they knew at least one crow had a part of this situation.

Luca was currently on the phone with Black Feather's Alpha, alerting him to the fact one of his members had gone rogue and warning the crows that any interference would be seen as an act of war and those involved would be put down as quickly as those who'd been directly involved in taking Luna.

Scottie was too busy watching the hawks, listening carefully to every single detail of the plans, and clinging to Jude's hand as though it were the last time she would feel the warmth of his skin against her own.

It very well could be the last time she held his hand, the very last time she looked into his beautiful eyes, the very last time she heard his voice.

And once again, she forced those thoughts away. They wouldn't help in battle. They would do nothing but distract her from what they needed to do to ensure Luna was brought home safely.

Lifting Jude's arm, she wrapped it around her shoulders and stepped closer to his side, drawing strength from the heat of his body.

He glanced down into her eyes as he spoke to the hawks and winked.

"I want someone to stay close to Scottie," he said.

"I will," Cohen said.

"I appreciate that. But someone on the ground needs to watch her back, as well."

"Are we really going through this again?" Campbell asked from a few feet away. "Any one of us can kick ass as well as you big, strong men. If she needs backup, one of us will be there. You birds need to keep any crows who come to the asshole's aid from divebombing us from the sky."

Scottie felt Jude's muscles tense under her touch, but he didn't argue with the human mate of Brax from Ravenwood. He knew there was no argument. Human or not, Campbell was a fierce fighter and had proven herself time and time again.

165

"You boys watch over us from the sky. Those of us with fur and claws will take on the hyenas," Scottie said, reaching up to pat Jude's chest.

"Fur, claws, and *guns*," Campbell corrected.

Scottie smiled at the woman. Of all the people she'd met, Campbell intrigued Scottie the most. The stories she'd heard nearly clashed with the person in front of her. Campbell was blunt and, at times, crass, but she was loyal, funny, and caring. She'd gone from believing all Shifters were the enemy to fighting for and alongside the same species she previously hated and feared.

Not to mention she'd fallen in love and mated with a panther Shifter.

As she looked around at the dozens of people, she realized there were so many stories, so much love, so many species who had come together to form a makeshift family who were more than willing to risk their own safety to protect a female. Scottie knew from the tales she'd been told they would have done the same thing whether Luna had been related to anyone or not. They had fought battles and wars with groups to earn the freedom of females, to prevent the forced pairings and Claimings that had been considered normal for so many centuries.

And every single person standing in the clearing shared matching looks of rage and determination.

There was no way they could lose. There was no way Luna wouldn't be returning home today. There was no way the enemy would win with the level of rage filling every Shifter waiting for the order to head out.

It would be an hour trip from Big River territory. The vampires and owls would join them halfway, joining the convoy of trucks and cars.

Excitement began to push away the anxiety and fear.

"Why are you smiling?" Jude asked, breaking through Scottie's thoughts.

"Look around," she said, waving a hand at the Shifters representing the various Packs, Clans, Prides, Parliaments, Covens, and Flocks.

Jude raised his eyes and scanned the clearing. A soft smile tugged at his lips.

"She'll be home by dinner."

"I wouldn't count on that," Jude said.

"Okay. But she'll be home before the day's out. Luna is coming home today. There are so many people willing to fight for her, to do anything and everything they have to to ensure she's returned to her Pride and her brother."

Jude placed his hands on her shoulders and turned her to face him. "Why do you sound jealous?" he asked with a hint of a frown.

"Not jealous. I'm in awe. Even when there were people in my life, they would have never..." She shook her head. "You have surrounded yourself with the most amazing people."

"They're your friends, too. Your family."

She nodded. "I know. That's why I'm smiling. No matter what happens, there will always be someone there. I'll never be alone again."

His frown turned half-hearted. "You plan on getting rid of me soon?"

Scottie shoved his shoulder. "You know what I meant. I have friends now. Cohen volunteered time after time to watch over me when you had to leave. He became a brother to me. And he never complained about his duties."

"Because you always have good snacks," Cohen mumbled.

Huffing a laugh, she shook her head and smiled. "Since you came into my life, I haven't felt alone. I haven't felt lonely. Not for a single second."

Jude pulled her into his arms, hugging her to his chest tightly and resting his cheek on the top of her head.

Scottie joined the females as they stripped and folded their clothing, leaving them in neat piles. The males didn't bother folding so much as their jeans, simply dropped everything to the forest floor.

It struck her as funny that, even though every single female there was mated and the men they loved were present, each group still separated to prevent the primal side of the males from accusing the unmated males of ogling their mate.

"You ready for this?" Campbell asked, the only female still fully dressed.

The human had guns in holsters on both hips as well knives in sheaths on each thigh.

"Yep," Scottie said.

Peyton and Emory Shifted the moment they were naked. Marisol waited until the other flight Shifters, including her family Parliament, were ready so they could all take to the sky at the same time.

The bears and panthers and wolves begged their mates to be careful before giving their bodies over to the animals.

The vampires…well, other than Everleigh, they creeped Scottie out. Their eyes glowed red and scanned the group, and she could have sworn they sneered a few times as though in disgust.

It didn't matter whether the vampires approved of fighting alongside Shifters or whether they felt the Shifters were inferior to their own kind, as long as they were there to help.

As each person dropped to their hands and knees to allow their animals to take over, the sounds of pops and cracks of bones breaking and reshaping filled the air and bounced off the trees around them.

Locking eyes on Jude, she smiled, mouthed *I love you*, then gave her body over to her mountain lion.

It was time. It was time to find Luna and get her home. It was time to punish the assholes who'd taken her. And, if they'd laid so much as a finger on her in the time she'd been their prisoner, she would enjoy watching Eli rip the perpetrators to pieces.

Jude's heart slammed against his ribs as he watched his beautiful mate Shift into her mountain lion, her tawny fur cast in gray and silver from the moonlight dappling through the trees.

He fucking hated this. He wanted to stay by her side when they rushed in. But his hawk would be no good hopping alongside. He needed to be up high with the rest of Skullbone and the Parliament of owls to keep an eye out for Black Feather or any others who might have been around to help the hyena.

There was no way it would be only one hyena and one crow. Hyenas would never roam alone. They would never pick a fight with anyone solo. Just like their wild cousins, they attacked in groups.

Cackles. A group of hyenas was called a Cackle. Even the name grated on Jude's fucking nerves.

He hated the fuckers. He'd also had no idea there were any in the area. These assholes were either nomads who'd wandered upon the area or had been called in by someone else.

Either way, they would end up the same way as any other rogue Shifter who'd dared lay a finger on an innocent female, especially one who happened to be related to a fucking Alpha.

Scottie's mountain lion glanced over her shoulder at Jude as she followed the rest of the predator Shifters through the woods. He couldn't stand the thought of losing sight of her, even for a moment.

With a thought, he gave his body over to his hawk and immediately flapped his wings, flying high above the trees, dipping and dodging branches to keep an eye on his mate.

When they would slow, he would land on a branch and split his attention between Scottie, the group, and the surrounding area, watching for any form of ambush or trap. He wouldn't put it past the hyenas to either be hiding in wait or to have snares hidden under leaves and brush.

Fuck. He didn't have a clear line of sight from this height. But he couldn't exactly skim along the forest floor. He would end up in the way of the massive creatures stalking toward the cabin hidden deep in the woods.

All he could do was hope that others had come to the same conclusion he had and would be watching closely, using their animal's preternaturally sharp vision to see even the smallest unnatural disturbance or pick up the scent of someone lurking nearby.

The steps of even the largest bear below were nearly silent. The wings of those flying high didn't so much as rustle the few stubborn leaves that clung to their branches. As long as there were no spies hiding and watching, they should arrive without warning and surprise the assholes holding Luna.

He refused to entertain the various ways she might have been hurt in her time away from her brother and her Pride. He refused to think that anyone would touch her or force themselves on her.

And, honestly, he pitied anyone who had anything to do with her abduction. Should Eli not be the one to rip the guilty party to shreds, the females would gladly take his place. Peyton alone wouldn't be stopped; her wolf's unstable manner would demand blood.

Luca circled around, tilting his head to look below before looking toward Jude. While the movies and books portrayed Shifters as some sort of telepathic creatures capable of communicating mentally in their animal forms, it wasn't true. And was, more often than not, a hindrance.

If they *had* been able to communicate, Jude could ask whether Luca had flown ahead and found the exact location of the cabin. He could let the others know whether any hyenas or other Shifters lingered nearby. He could alert them to whether they would require the vampires' assistance.

The vampires followed at a distance. They were reluctant participants and would only join forces if it was needed to keep Everleigh safe. Otherwise, they would remain out of sight until it was over.

That was fine. In Jude's eyes, this was a Shifter problem and should be dealt with by fellow Shifters. But that didn't mean he wasn't grateful to the intriguing yet creepy creatures for their presence.

Watching Scottie a few more seconds, he jerked his attention to Luca when he dove directly in front of him. Telepathy wasn't needed; it was obvious the newly appointed Alpha wanted Jude and the rest of the hawks to follow.

Both sides of Jude warred with the need to stay near their mate while also needing to follow their Alpha. It was obvious Luca needed the Flock to see something. He could have been sending out a warning, he could have the location.

But Jude wouldn't know if he didn't join the rest of Skullbone.

Fighting the urge to ignore Luca and stay near Scottie, he spread his wings and glided on the wind, following the others as they headed further into the woods.

The scent of wood smoke rose on the air a few moments before a slender tendril appeared just above the tree line. Where there was smoke…

As though they'd rehearsed it, the Flock separated, staying hidden within the trees as they surveyed the area below them. There were two four-wheelers parked in front of the cabin and several males walking around outside. They looked as though they were on guard.

Were they anticipating an attack or were they simply being cautious?

Once again, the inability to communicate with those below or even those flying beside him was a major hindrance and could be dangerous. When he was the Alpha, when his life was the only one on the line, Jude had never had a problem flying beak first into danger.

But not only was his beautiful mate stalking through the woods below him, but nearly every single one of his friends were there, as well. His family. The people he cared for most in the world were creeping closer to what could end up as a trap.

What the fuck could he do? If he made a single noise to alert those below, the hyenas and any others who might have been aiding them would be made aware of the approach.

But if he said nothing, and there were more of the enemy hiding in wait nearby…

Fuck.

The only saving grace for him at the moment was that he was no longer in charge. It was Luca's responsibility to lead the Flock, to determine their next move.

That also meant the safety of Jude's mate was in Luca's hands.

Luca dipped and rotated his body, staying far enough above the tree line to stay out of sight of the hyenas. The rest of the hawks followed, coasting on the breeze until they were directly above the large group of varying Shifter species.

Jude caught Scottie's upward glance and felt a surge of pride. Her mountain lion didn't falter a step. There was no fear in her eyes. She simply continued stalking forward, pushing forward until she was in the middle of the males instead of lingering back with the females.

Jude still wasn't keen on the fact a human female had joined, but also knew none of the males would ever order their mates to do anything, even if that meant staying back when there was a fight.

He knew Scottie would have never stayed back. It didn't matter whether he begged and pleaded, whether he ordered her or even left someone like Cohen behind to watch over her. She would have literally fought tooth and nail to be there on the front line, determined to help in any way she could.

As much as the thought of her in a fight terrified him, it also made him admire her more. His mate was more than he could have dreamed, more than he deserved. She was everything he could ever want in a female and partner in life.

Eli and Gray were the first in the line. Both stopped and lifted their heads. It didn't appear as though they were searching the skies. Rather, they were scenting the air. Hopefully, they could detect the number of males the hawks had seen from the sky.

He was sure there were more than what could be seen. Jude knew there would be others inside if not nearby. No way would the few hyenas below be prepared to give up easily and no way would they fight with honor.

But this group wouldn't give up. Whether Eli fell while trying to rescue his sister, every single person beside and behind him would fight until their last breath to ensure she was returned home. Then they would spend every minute needed to help her return to some form of normalcy.

First, they had to find Luna. If she wasn't being held in the cabin, they would be back to square one.

As the hawks floated on the breeze, the Parliament of owls flanked them, silently flapping their wings and landing in a tree ahead of the group. They, like the vampires, would only enter the fight if needed. Jude was only barely familiar with Marisol's parents. And Marisol was so sweet and quiet, he hated to think of the small female fighting the crows if they should enter the fray.

A sound touched Jude's ears. The entirety of the predator Shifters below halted their steps, their ears twitching as the same sound made it to them.

Leaves crunched ahead. Whatever was making the sound was light and hurried, not the heavy footfalls of a large Shifter or adult male.

Jude's hawk tilted its head, trying to see through the limbs, trying to see into the dark.

No one moved. No one charged forward.

And then a burst of motion beside Jude caused the hawks to dive toward the ground.

Cohen was in his human form a second before he crashed to the ground, his body hitting hard and rolling before he lunged to his feet and sprinted forward.

What the hell was he doing? Cohen never broke rank. He stayed in line and did as his Alpha ordered. With the exception of when he alerted Scottie to his presence.

The hawks followed, staying barely above the Shifters as they rushed forward.

And then the source of those soft footfalls came into focus.

Luna limped forward at an awkward half-jog. Her arms were wrapped around her middle as she squinted into the dark.

When Cohen got closer to her, she instantly threw up her arms and balled her hands into fists, prepared to fight. The sight of a male as large and naked as Cohen would cause anyone to react with fear. Especially one who'd been taken from her home and her family.

"Easy," Cohen said, holding his hands in front of him before quickly dropping them and shielding his junk from her eyes.

Eli rushed past Cohen, nearly plowing over him to get to his sister.

"Eli?" she asked, her voice shaky.

The large lion slowed and ran his large body along her side, a sound that was half growl and half purr rumbling from his chest.

Scottie grunted as she pushed her animal back and reclaimed her skin. "Are you Luna?"

Luna frowned in Scottie's direction then her eyes seemed to focus. She finally saw the large army of fur ahead of her and her bottom lip quivered.

"Yes," she said on a sob.

"Are you okay?"

The female looked over her shoulder, lifting an arm and pointing in the opposite direction. "They're coming."

"What?" Scottie asked.

"They were distracted, so I broke out a window and climbed out. They're coming."

The fuckers were on their way to retrieve her. They would chase her down.

A second after Luna had warned them, the sound of four wheelers rumbled to life and leaves crunched under paws as the hyenas took their animal forms to track Luna.

Why hadn't she Shifted? Her lioness could have run much faster, put a lot more space between herself and the fuckers at the cabin. She would have scented her brother and those who were searching for her.

A long, low growl rumbled up from Eli's throat a split second before his muscles bunched and he exploded forward. Nearly all those who'd joined to track Luna followed him, rushing headlong into the fight.

Jude looked to each of the hawks.

"We go," Luca said, hunching forward and giving his body back to his hawk before launching into the sky.

Cohen shook his head. "I'm staying. I'm not leaving her unprotected."

"I'll stay, too," Scottie said.

A few other females stayed behind but remained Shifted in case the fight made it to them.

With a quick look at Scottie, Jude let his hawk push forward and joined the hawks and others. He didn't go far.

The hyenas were barely fifty yards from where Luna stumbled upon her rescuers. This had to be stopped now. Jude wouldn't let anyone get near his mate, wouldn't let anyone take Luna again, wouldn't let any of these mother fuckers get anywhere near the females who circled the injured lioness.

Chapter Sixteen

Scottie positioned herself so she was between Luna and the sound of the enemy approaching.

"Can you Shift?" Cohen asked.

"I've been trying since they showed up in Hope territory. My lioness refuses to come forward."

A tear fell over her lashes and trailed down her cheek, leaving a streak in the dirt smeared on her cheeks.

All their clothes were in piles several hundred yards back. There was nothing to wrap around her shoulders to warm her.

"Did they…" Scottie couldn't force herself to form the words.

But Luna caught on. Shaking her head, she lifted a hand and pushed her hair from her face.

"No. Just…no. They didn't hurt me like that."

The rumble of the four-wheelers cut off, but the sounds of leaves and twigs cracking and crunching mixed with snarls, growls, and howls of both anger and pain. All Scottie could do was pray that none of those sounds of pain came from any of her people.

A few of the females who remained crouched low and growled or hissed, their ears pressed back as their eyes scanned the dark ahead of them.

The sounds were growing closer. And Luna was too injured to Shift or run.

"We need to get you to the vehicles," Scottie said.

Wrapping an arm around Luna's back, Scottie turned her and urged her forward, their steps slow as she struggled to put weight on her left foot.

Before Scottie or Luna had time to say a word, Cohen scooped her into his arms and took off at a sprint, carrying her back to the vehicles.

Scottie jogged to catch up until a loud squawk filled the air. That was definitely a sound from one of the hawks.

Oh no.

Turning, she stared in the direction where her mate and the others had rushed to cut off the approach of the hyenas.

She shouldn't leave Luna. She should stay with Cohen to keep her safe in case one of the hyenas were able to break off and get to her.

But she couldn't stand the thought of something happening to Jude while she stayed safely by the trucks and SUVs and cars.

Turning back, she could no longer see Cohen or Luna. And the females who remained appeared to look to her for direction.

Scottie wasn't familiar enough with everyone yet to know who was still there, which of the females had what animal inside of them. But none of them looked afraid or like they would rather stay back or retreat with Cohen and Luna.

Opening her mouth, Scottie released a war cry that morphed into her animal's roar when another squawk rent through the air. She would not allow any of the Flock to be injured or killed if she could help.

Without bothering to see who was following, she dug her claws into the forest floor, pushing herself forward as fast as her legs would go. Within seconds, she plowed headlong into the fight, using her animal's body like a bowling bowl to knock over two hyenas who were attempting to overcome a female wolf.

There were far more of the hyenas than her group had anticipated. Although her friends had made sure to bring plenty of backup, both on the ground and in the sky.

The vampires were still nowhere to be seen. All she could do was hope they would step in if the time came where their help was needed. She assumed they would at least keep Everleigh safe.

She and Campbell were the only two who weren't in animal form. Campbell was the only human present, though she was armed to the teeth and could fight with her fists and feet as well as any MMA champ she'd seen on TV.

Everleigh…well, she was a vampire. Scottie wasn't sure whether the female had any special gifts like the others she'd heard about, but assumed she was capable of taking care of herself since her giant of a mate hadn't demanded she stay back with the mothers of the small children.

Taking a second to survey the area, her heart clenched when she spotted two hawks unmoving on the ground. She had no idea which two they were and whether they were injured…or dead.

Please not Jude.

Dodging hyenas and a couple of crows who dove at her face, she made it to where the hawks were and used her snout to push at the unmoving bodies, inhaling their scent deep into her lungs. Flight Shifters didn't carry the same scent the way predator Shifters did, but she didn't pick up anything that indicated her mate was one of the two whose lives were lost.

It seemed unfair that they died in their animal forms and would be buried as hawks. Similar to when all those crows had died in her yard. She assumed she should be thankful the members of Skullbone wouldn't be piled up the way the crows from Black Feather had that day.

Jude was still somewhere in the sky. There weren't nearly as many crows as they'd feared. Which Scottie had to assume meant Black Feather wasn't fully behind the hyenas' actions; rather, a small group had gone rogue.

At least she really hoped that was all that was happening. Otherwise, a lot more crows would be arriving soon and more lives would be lost.

Still unsure of who each of the bears or wolves or panthers were, she only knew they were on her side and focused her attention on the hyenas who appeared to have multiplied since she'd entered the field. Shit. Were there not enough fighters on her side?

Wings flapped overhead, growls and snarls mixed with the sound as the scent of blood grew more pungent, the coppery scent teasing her senses until her cat began to grow unsteady with a rush of blood lust.

Teeth flashing, she lunged at the first person she found, latching onto the hyena's throat and shaking with all her might.

Unfortunately, the Shifter male was nearly twice her size and easily bucked her off.

Rebounding quickly, Scottie's cat once more lunged, hooking her long, razor sharp claws into his back as she clamped her mouth around his neck, kicking at him with her back legs as she tightened her grip with both paws and her maw.

The moment the tips of her fangs pierced flesh and blood filled her mouth, Scottie's beast was in ecstasy. The reasons for the fight were no longer important. Her animal wanted more, more blood, more violence, more death.

The moment the hyena went limp in her grip, she dropped him and sought another victim.

Claws ripped at her ears, but she simply reared back and swatted at the crow overhead and turned her attention to a hyena squaring up with a tiny female wolf.

He would die. Scottie's cat would be the one to end him.

Even as Scottie screamed inside her cat's head to calm down, to focus, to find Jude, her animal ignored its human side and lunged.

Jude's heart ached in his chest. The brothers, Tony and Cal, laid lifeless side by side on the ground. They'd attempted to dive at the hyenas and had been struck down. Deep slashes across Tony's throat and Cal's abdomen seeped the last of their lifeblood onto the forest floor.

It had been years since they'd lost a member of Skullbone. Though Jude was no longer the Alpha, he still felt the excruciating pain of failure and loss. He had led these males for so long, had thought of them as family for a decade.

Truly, the only upside to the loss was that the brothers died together and wouldn't have to live their lives grieving the other.

But the rest of the hawks would mourn their loss. Their absence would be felt like a dagger in the heart.

Tilting his head, Jude checked on Scottie. She was attacking a pair of hyenas, squaring off with both, her muzzle and tawny fur covered and matted with blood. He had no idea how much was hers and how much belonged to the enemy.

There were scratches along her ears and the top of her head as though a crow had attempted to latch onto her face and blind her. But his mate had avoided losing her sight.

As he dipped again, his heart stuttered when a third hyena joined his friends against Scottie. Where the fuck were they all coming from? The intel he'd received from the vampires and the quick surveillance he and the hawks had done didn't show more than a dozen. Yet there were at least twenty still fighting and several others lying dead on the ground.

Why? Why had they taken Luna? Why were they congregating so close to Cedar Hill? Hyenas were natural enemies to lions in the wild, but, as far as Jude knew, Eli hadn't earned any enemies in his time as Alpha of Hope Pride.

Hell. Jude wasn't even aware the hyenas were in the area. He wondered if any of the others had heard tale of their move to the area.

Before Jude could dive into the fray and even the playing field, Zeke's monstrous bear charged forward and ripped two of the hyenas away. Eli finished off the hyena he was fighting and turned to the next.

One by one, the hyenas' numbers began to dwindle. Everleigh drained one, her fangs sunk deep into its throat. Emory and Peyton teamed up to take out another. Reed was toying with one of them, bouncing around like a pup before ending the hyena's life.

The few crows who'd been in the sky were either dead or had retreated when they realized their fight was lost.

With no birds to fight in the sky, Jude could focus his attention on his mate. He might not have been as valuable in the fight as the large predator Shifters, but he sure as fuck could use his talons to rip the eyes from anyone who attempted to attack Scottie.

As the number of hyenas dwindled, Jude watched as Scottie's lion sought its next victim.

And then she turned on one of the panthers. *Shit.*

Wings expanded, he coasted to the forest floor and pushed his hawk back until he was standing naked in the middle of his friends.

"Scottie!" he yelled.

But she either didn't hear him or wasn't paying enough attention. Or, worst case scenario, her mountain lion had taken full control and refused to allow its human counterpart to so much as acknowledge their mate.

"Damn it," he muttered, not bothering to cover himself as he made his way through the few people still fighting.

As he'd hoped, his people had come out the victors. Other than the brothers from Skullbone, he would have to wait until they were safely at home to learn whether or not they'd lost any more friends.

Gripping Scottie's mountain lion by the scruff and attempting to subdue her, he turned her so she could see his face. But she swiped out, nearly slashing her claws across Jude's chest.

"Scottie!" he yelled, giving the mountain lion a shake.

A blur of gray and black fur entered his vision a split second before Scottie was yanked from his grasp. A large female wolf had Scottie's cat pinned to the ground, its fangs inches from Scottie's face as it growled long and low.

Peyton. Peyton was either defending Jude or trying to calm Scottie's animal enough for her human side to push forward.

It took several agonizing seconds of Scottie's beast struggling against Peyton before she slowly relaxed and rolled onto her back, exposing her belly in submission.

When Peyton's wolf was content there would be no further attacks, she stepped away, but kept her teeth bared and watched.

"Scottie," Jude repeated. "It's over. The battle is over. Come back."

She hissed once, but, in a slow and painful Shift, she pushed her animal back until she laid naked on the ground.

"Fuck," she muttered. "What the hell was that?"

Peyton turned and trotted back to where others had Shifted back to their human forms and checked on each other. There were a lot of injuries, but Jude had no idea whether they'd lost anyone other than Tony and Cal. That loss alone cut like a knife.

But they needed to round up their people and leave this area. Just because they'd annihilated the hyenas who'd been present didn't mean there weren't more nearby or on their way. Another battle while so many of them were badly injured could end in disaster.

Hand cupping his junk, Jude lowered to his knees beside Scottie. "Are you alright?"

"That hurt," she grumbled as she pushed to a sitting position.

Every single Shifter who'd returned to their human form stood around naked and bleeding. But that didn't stop his urge to shield her body from any male who might look in her direction.

"I couldn't get her to stop. It was like she didn't hear me. Or refused to listen. She was…she went a little psycho."

"Blood lust," he said, running his hand over her head and pushing her hair away from her face.

He checked over every inch of her body that he could see, looking for any injuries that might require Zeke's medical knowledge and skills. But the superficial wounds he spotted on the top of her head and across her forehead would heal within a few days.

"Is Luna okay?" she asked.

Jude stood and offered her his hand, helping her to her feet.

"I haven't seen her since Cohen took off with her," he said, turning her to check for any more cuts or gashes on her back.

She'd come out of the fight nearly untouched.

"Fuck!" Luca bellowed.

Scottie turned in the direction of the sound. Her face fell as she turned her eyes up to Jude's face. "Oh no."

Wrapping an arm around her shoulders, Jude led her to where the rest of the Flock gathered around Cal's and Tony's bodies. They were still in their hawk form. Unlike the movies, Shifters didn't return to their human form after death. They remained in whatever state they were in when they lost their lives.

Luca dropped to his knees and touched each of the hawks. Whether he was saying goodbye or checking for any evidence of life Jude didn't know. But when the new Alpha sat back on his haunches, tears welled in his eyes and streaked down his cheeks. He didn't swipe them away, didn't try to hide them.

Jude had endured this type of loss only once. And he remembered the crushing feeling, the feeling of utter loss and failure.

But Luca had failed no one. If blame should have been placed on anyone it would be the fuckers who'd taken Luna. It was the assholes who'd gathered for whatever reason, for some unknown vendetta.

Burke lowered and lifted Cal's hawk into his arms, cradling him carefully against his chest. Luca did the same with Tony. They would return them to Skullbone territory where they would be laid to rest. They would mourn the loss of the males, mourn the loss of their friends.

Everyone began to return to the vehicles they'd left parked, the mood somber as the hawks carried their fallen brothers. They would normally celebrate, meet at Moe's for beer.

Not tonight.

Tonight, everyone would return home to their families and hold them closer.

"Were there any other losses?" Scottie asked softly.

The vampires hadn't even made an appearance, which Everleigh wasn't happy about based on the fury in her blood red eyes.

"None from Ravenwood," Aron answered.

"None from Big River," Reed said.

"None from Blackwater," Carter answered.

It went on like that from Morse and the owls, confirming only the hawks had lost two of their own.

Chapter Seventeen

Three weeks after the battle in the woods, the mood had barely improved. Scottie's heart hurt for Jude. Her heart hurt for all the hawks. Cohen had barely darkened her stoop whether Jude had to leave for the afternoon or not. Although that might have had something to do with the fact that they'd both started jobs together with the bears from Blackwater Clan.

Luca had taken the loss of the brothers hard. He'd disappeared for four days after his hawk had burst free and taken flight. She and the rest of Skullbone had tilted their heads back and watched as he spread his wings and floated on the breeze before disappearing from sight far above the trees.

When he'd come back, he was quiet, subdued, and sad. So sad. Scottie constantly invited him and the others to her and Jude's home, but they had only accepted once, using the weather as their excuse for staying in their own territory.

It would take time. She'd suffered in silence for years after each personal loss whether because someone walked away or lost their lives. Hopefully, Luca's heart would heal faster and wouldn't harden. He was a nice guy. She wanted to see him and the others happy again.

Jude was quiet, as well. He was still affectionate toward her, still touched her as though she were the most precious thing in the world, but the loss of Tony and Cal had left a dark place in everyone's hearts.

Scottie had only visited with Luna twice since she'd been returned home. She hadn't met her before, but could tell she wasn't behaving as herself. The lionesses stayed near her at all times, hovering near anytime a visitor arrived in Hope Pride territory.

Except when Scottie arrived with Cohen. She couldn't say for sure, but it sure as hell appeared as though Luna and Cohen had formed an odd friendship. The female obviously felt comfortable and safe around him since he'd carried her through the woods and away from the hyenas.

It could also have been because Cohen was so sweet and open and kind. Scottie had felt connected to him and viewed him as a brother within days of meeting him.

Rolling onto her side, Scottie stared at Jude's profile. His eyes were closed, but she could tell by his breathing he was no longer sleeping.

"Are you going to be okay?" she asked.

She felt like she'd asked that same question so many times since that night. And no matter how many times he tried to convince her he was fine she could see the anguish in his eyes.

Lids still closed, he rolled over and tugged her closer until their bodies were pressed together and her cheek rested against his chest. She listened to the steady thump of his heart and let her eyes drift closed.

"I thought it would be easier when I was no longer Alpha," he admitted.

They hadn't discussed the battle since that night. They hadn't talked about his abdication in weeks. They'd barely discussed the loss of the members of Skullbone. He'd gone quiet, and she was doing her best to give him space to grieve and recover while letting him know she was there if he needed to talk or vent or cry.

"Alpha or not, they were your friends," she said.

His arms wrapped around her and hugged her tightly.

"Is Luca going to be okay?"

He released a frustrated growl deep in his throat. "It'll take a while, but he'll heal. Losing a member of the Flock on your watch…it can fuck with your head."

She nodded, his chest hair tickling her cheek. "I can't even imagine."

She knew how it felt to lose people but had never been the one in charge of keeping others safe.

Tightening her arms around his waist, she nuzzled her cheek closer, inhaling his scent and sighing. "Are *we* going to be okay?" she asked.

She understood loss and she understood grief. But the fear of him losing so much of himself that he no longer felt the same about her caused that old feeling of abandonment to rear its ugly head.

Jude pulled back and frowned down into her face. "What do you mean? Of course we're okay."

She shrugged slightly. "You've been a little distant. I mean, I know you still love me and all, but I feel like I'm watching you disappear."

Pushing up until he was in a sitting position, he hovered over her when she rolled onto her back to look up into his face.

"I'm sorry," he said, dragging a fingertip down her cheek. "I know I've been...it's been a long time since the Flock has lost anyone. And I feel like I've failed them." He held up his hand when she opened her mouth to argue or protest. "I know I didn't fail them. And neither did Luca. But it's how I feel right now. And why I've been...I don't know, distant. I'm sorry."

"It'll take time," she said, pushing up onto her elbows.

His eyes dipped to her bare breasts and, even during such a heavy moment, she felt her body grow warm from his simple glance.

Reaching down, she pulled the sheet up until she was fully covered so neither of them would be distracted.

"Take the time you need, but don't disappear. I'll be here for whatever you need."

A ghost of a smile tilted up the corners of his lips. "I love you, Scottie."

"I know," she teased, then squealed when he poked a finger into her ribs.

"Let's get out of the house," he said.

Her brows shot up her forehead. "Really?"

The only time they'd left in the past three weeks was to either check in with the hawks or to check on Luna. And that had only been three times...in three freaking weeks. They'd left the house three times out of over twenty-one days.

"Yeah. I need to get out of this funk. See some friends. Check on everyone else."

"Moe's?"

He shrugged and nodded.

With an excited squeal, she tossed the blankets off her legs and lunged to her feet. "Text everyone. I want to see them all. Including

185

Luca. Make sure he comes out. Don't give him a choice; pull Alpha rank if you have to."

"I'm not the Alpha anymore."

"I don't care. Do you what you have to to get him out. And Luna. She needs to be out with friends."

"You've turned into quite the social butterfly," he teased when she began to pull clean clothes from the dresser drawer and her closet.

"I will never be considered a social butterfly. But we all need to be together. We need to bond and remember why we fight."

She wasn't sure she'd ever said something so deep or poetic, but she'd meant every word. If they continued to keep their distance from each other, they might grow apart. And she had grown fond of the people Jude considered friends and family. Even if Peyton *had* dominated her that night.

Well, Peyton's wolf had dominated Scottie's mountain lion. And Scottie's animal deserved it. Her freaking beast had gone feral and nearly attacked Jude.

She hurried to the bathroom and showered, then dried off and ran a brush through her hair. She didn't bother with makeup, didn't bother blow drying her hair. It was time to be among her friends, among her people, among her new family.

And it was time for them to all to start healing. They couldn't do that if they all shut down and locked themselves away in their homes.

Jude passed her in the hallway. And he hadn't bothered to dress or carry any clean clothes with him.

Stopping in her tracks, she dragged her eyes from his head to his toes and back up again.

If he didn't get in that bathroom and close the door, they were going to be delayed…by a lot. Because the sight of her mate's amazing body sent heat coursing through her body.

Towel wrapped around her sarong style, she gripped it tightly and turned away from him, giggling an extremely girly sound when he swatted her ass as she passed.

That was one of the things she'd missed the past few weeks, that teasing, flirtatious side of him. While she understood the heavy mood, she was still happy to see his other side peeking through.

By the time he stepped into the bedroom – still butt naked – Scottie was dressed and sliding her feet into socks.

"You're killing me," she said, dropping her eyes to her shoes when he passed by her, his ass and cock so close all she had to do was reach up and she could touch him.

And stroke him.

And drag his body down to hers so she could feel his weight pressing her into the mattress as he slid into her.

With a very human growl of frustration, she shoved to her feet and carried her shoes into the living room, the sound of Jude's chuckles following her from the room.

It had taken some coaxing, but all the hawks from Skullbone joined them at Moe's, as well as a majority of the wolves, panthers, bears, and other species from Big River, Blackwater, Ravenwood, and Morse. The only friends missing were those who had small children to care for at home.

It wasn't uncommon for the Shifters to bring their pups or cubs to the bar, but the day was getting later, which meant the place would soon get fuller. Noah always made everyone put out their cigarettes and watch their language when kids were present, but that didn't mean there wouldn't be a few outbursts of chaos.

Luca remained silent as the crowd chatted and laughed, although the banter wasn't as light and easy as usual. It was obvious a pall had fallen over them after the Flock had lost two of its members. It had been so damn long since any of them had lost any of their people that it felt alien. Wrong.

What surprised Jude was how closely Luna sat beside Cohen. Or the fact she had come out at all. And that Eli had actually left Hope Pride to join Skullbone at Moe's. They'd been together at the bar when his sister had been taken.

Then again, there were still members of Big River Pack who stayed behind. Gray and Nova stayed with their daughter. Reed and Lola stayed behind with theirs. And Micah and Callie stayed behind with the little boy they'd taken in and loved like their own. So, technically, the only members of Big River who wouldn't be there if Hope Pride needed assistance were Peyton and Tristan since Emory was technically no longer a member of Big River.

As Scottie leaned into his side, he lifted his arm and wrapped it around her shoulders, pressing a kiss to her forehead when she smiled up at him.

"This is better, right?" she whispered low enough for only him to hear over the music and conversation.

He nodded and lowered his head to taste her lips. "Much better," he agreed when he pulled away.

The conversation might have been forced and subdued but at least they were all together. They were smiling. Luca was in his human form and among his friends. It would take longer than three weeks for them to grieve the loss of Cal and Tony, but life would eventually go on. It always did. It always would.

As badly as he hurt over the loss, he had Scottie by his side. He would always have her at his side. She'd been his rock, silently sitting with him when he didn't feel like talking, running her fingers through his hair when he felt at his lowest as though she could sense it.

Country music played through the speakers attached near the ceiling, pool balls clicked on the table near the back, various conversations hummed around him.

The door opened. Noah turned his attention to greet the newcomers then tensed.

"What the fuck are you doing here? Not welcome, asshole."

The entirety of the bar went silent, the only sound was a man singing about a lost love to an acoustic guitar.

All heads turned toward the small group who'd entered, ignoring Noah and scanning the crowd until their focus zeroed in on Luca and the other members of Skullbone Flock.

"Did you hear me? Get the fuck out," Noah grumbled as he rounded the bar.

Luca pushed to his feet, followed by Jude, Cohen, Burke, and even Scottie. Then, one by one, every single friend who'd met up for the night pushed to their feet and prepared for a full out bar brawl.

"We need to talk," Dane said, his attention solely on Jude.

Luca stepped forward. "I'm Alpha."

The Alpha of Black Feather frowned deeply, his eyes bouncing from Jude to Luca then back again.

Jude nodded.

"We had nothing to do with that shit. With the female being taken," Dane said to Luca.

"There were crows fighting alongside the hyenas."

Dane glanced back at one of the males who stood to his left. Stepping forward, the male kept his eyes lowered from Luca's face.

"I was one of those who joined the hyenas."

Growls erupted throughout the room as the air become pungent with the scent of fur. It wouldn't take much for several Shifters to explode from their skin and fill the room with massive beasts.

Luca stepped forward, flanked by Jude and Burke. Eli pushed through the crowd and stormed forward. It took three members of Blackwater and one of the panthers to stop him from ripping the head off the crow.

The few members of Black Feather who had arrived stepped forward, prepared to protect their member if needed.

Dane held up a hand. "He's here to apologize and offer an explanation."

"What fucking explanation could there be for stealing my sister?" Eli roared, the sound irritating Jude's sensitive ears.

"My sister," the crow said.

He lifted both arms as he stepped forward, either to attempt to appear as though he wasn't an immediate threat or to keep his Crew from following.

"Flight Shifters are male," Scottie said. "Right?"

No one answered her. There had been incidents in the past of various flight Shifters being born female, but it was rare and few between. He had never personally met a female hawk or crow in his lifetime.

The crow's eyes flitted to Scottie only briefly before returning to Luca. "I either handed over one of the lionesses, or they would take my sister. I know what I did was fucked up, but my sister…" The male shook his head. "She's not strong. She's not a fighter. She would never have survived being taken by the hyenas."

"Why didn't you just come to us?"

Dane snorted derisively. "Because our groups have always gotten along so well."

"We have always done everything in our power to protect females. We could have helped," Luca said.

Jude might still have had an issue with stepping down and might still have had a hard time conceding to someone else, but Luca was doing well, even if the loss of the two members had hit him hard.

A muscle in the male's cheek jumped. He turned to look at his Alpha before turning back to the hawks.

"I didn't want anyone to know she existed. Only a few of the crows in Black Feather knew about her."

"You didn't trust your own people?"

The male opened his mouth, but a hand clamped around his arm.

"Niko," the male gripping his arm muttered, the tone of his voice full of warning.

Niko shrugged from his Crew brother and shot him a look. "I didn't trust the former Alpha. And there are still some who think like Clint. I trust the males here with me now."

Jude turned to gauge the reaction of his Flock and his friends. All were still tense, but Eli was no longer struggling against their hold.

"Why did the hyenas want a lioness?" Luca asked.

"Because the fuckers wanted to breed her. Wanted to mix blood."

"Since when do they give a shit about lions?" Eli asked.

Dane shrugged. "If lions and hyenas are enemies in the wild, maybe the dumbasses thought you should be enemies, as well."

There hadn't been a lot of interaction between Dane, the crows, and Skullbone other than the airborne skirmish the day he'd crashed onto Scottie's yard, at least not since Clint had been taken out of the picture.

Honestly, Jude didn't know much about Dane and had assumed he'd be as heartless and dishonest as the former Alpha.

Perhaps it was time they truly spent time hashing out the past bull shit so both groups could move forward. Although, Dane needed to spend time weeding out any fuckers who had the same mindset as Clint, if what Niko had said was true.

Until that time, Jude would remain untrusting of anyone who flew under the Black Feather name.

"Why are you here telling us this?" Luca asked.

"I didn't want any part of it. I didn't want the female..." Niko's eyes darted over Jude's shoulder, presumably at where Luna sat surrounded by large males. "I'm sorry." His eyes stayed on Luna as he dipped his head.

The words sounded genuine, but it would take more than simple words to aid in the healing. Not only had Luna suffered trauma, but the Flock had lost two hawks.

"Where is your sister now?" Luca asked.

"That doesn't matter."

"It does."

"Why?" Niko asked, his brows slamming together.

"Is she in a safe location?"

"She's safe. And will remain that way. She's, uh...she's safe," Niko said.

There was definitely something Niko was hiding. But that was something for Luca to dig into, something for the Alpha of Skullbone to discuss with the Alpha of Black Feather.

This was yet another time Jude was thankful he'd walked away from the role. Luca had a whole new stack of shit to unpack and resolve.

"Other than Niko, the crows who sided with the hyenas have been dealt with," Dane said.

"Dealt with how?" Luca asked.

"Every single one of them better be dead," Eli demanded.

"A few were put down. The others were exiled. Niko is the only remaining member of the...incident?"

"The incident?" Eli said, his voice a deep, intimidating growl. "They kidnapped my sister knowing the hyenas intended to breed her against her will."

"I wouldn't have let that happen," Niko said.

191

"You could have come to us," Luca repeated. "We could have helped your sister."

Both sides were quiet a few moments. Dane nodded once, then motioned for his Crew to file out of the bar.

"That's it?" Eli said, attempting to follow the males outside, but was once again held back. "You fuck with my sister and I'm supposed to let it go because you apologized?"

The crows didn't stop their retreat, didn't say anything else. Niko stopped at the door and looked as though he wanted to say something, but shook his head, dropped it, and stepped out into the cold night air.

Chapter Eighteen

A female crow. Holy cow. Or Scottie supposed she could say holy crow.

"I thought you said flight Shifters were super rare," she said to Jude as they changed out of the clothes they'd worn to Moe's.

She would have to toss them in the wash first thing in the morning. It wasn't so bad during the day, but a visit to the bar in the evening always made her feel like she reeked of cigarette smoke when she left.

"They are. I can understand why that Niko dude would keep his sister hidden."

"But he didn't have the right to side with the hyenas."

Jude shook his head as he tossed his shirt into the hamper. "Absolutely not. I could almost understand if they'd already taken her. He wouldn't be the first male to work with assholes in hopes of earning his sister's freedom. But it sounds like the hyenas hadn't come anywhere near his sister. He volunteered to help nab a lioness. He's still as guilty as the fuckers who were behind the whole thing."

Scottie threw her dirty clothes into the hamper on top of Jude's and tugged on a tank top and some sleep pants. She bobbed her head side to side.

"Is he, though?"

Jude turned an incredulous look to Scottie. "You saying he's not guilty?"

They each pulled their side of the blankets down on the bed and climbed in. She couldn't hold in the smile at how domestic and natural the whole thing felt. Barely a month of cohabitation, barely a month of being mated and she felt as though the two of them had known each other every minute of the entire lives.

"Not at all. What he did was screwed up. But think about it for a second. Put yourself in his shoes. What if it were me—"

Jude held a hand up. "Nope. At no point would you ever be in a position where I would need to sacrifice another female. And I love you. You know I do. More than I have ever loved another person. But no way would I offer up an innocent female in exchange. My own life or freedom, in a heartbeat. Not a female, though."

She knew that to be true. Honestly, she wasn't sure why she would think he or any of his friends would sacrifice anyone but themselves whether the person at risk was their mate or not.

"Did something else seem off about that conversation?"

Jude rolled onto his side and propped his head on his head. "The entire thing was off."

"He said something about his sister not being a fighter or strong enough or whatever. Like there was more to it than simply protecting her."

Jude shrugged up his free shoulder. "Who knows? I'm sure he and Dane were hiding a shitload from us."

Scottie laid down, resting her head on the pillow and staring up into Jude's face. "So, what now?" she asked.

A confused frown created a crease between his dark blond brows. She fought the urge to smooth the crease with her fingertip.

"What do you mean?"

"Luna's back at home. The brothers have been laid to rest. Everyone is doing their best to heal from all the trauma and loss. So...what now?"

"I'm still not sure what you're asking."

She pushed up onto her elbows. "Well, you got a job you seem to like. Between the two of us, we've got a bit of money stashed away. So...I was tossing something around in my head."

"What?"

Her cheeks heated as she organized the plan in her head and figured out how to articulate it without sounding silly.

"I was just thinking after a few more months, we'll have a lot more money saved up. Then we could buy more property and build some bigger houses for the hawks."

His frown disappeared and his brows raised. "You want to move?"

She couldn't quite shrug in her position so she tilted her head a bit. "I thought it might be easier to have all the hawks together, closer...for when we have a family together. Then our cubs will have a bunch of uncles to watch over them."

Jude's eyes darted to her stomach. "Are you...?"

Huffing a laugh, she sat up fully. "No. No," she said quickly, stopping him before he got too excited. "But...I don't know. I could always cut my work load or set my hours for when you were home. Then one of us will always be with our baby. If you were ready to start a family."

"Are you serious?" he asked, his voice barely above a whisper.

She nodded.

"I mean, are you serious about all of it? About moving to a larger property so Skullbone can build bigger houses and about starting a family."

"Yes and yes. I just got to thinking maybe if the guys were around a cub –"

"Or chick—"

"That they might be more open to finding their own mate and maybe starting a family. With bigger houses and with all of us living close together, we can all help each other like they do in Big River."

Tears actually glistened in Jude's eyes a second before he practically tackled her to the mattress, his arms tight around her as he hugged her to his body in a crushing hug.

"I love you, Scottie. I love you so much."

"I love you, too."

Thank you for reading ***Jude's Rescue***. I hope you loved Jude and Scottie as much as I do! If you liked this book, please consider rating or reviewing it on Amazon and/or Goodreads. Your support will help other readers find the panthers, bears, wolves, and more of Cedar Hill! **Thank you!**

To get early news, free short stories, and vote for stories, make sure to subscribe to my newsletter. Don't worry, I promise not to spam your inbox! You can subscribe at www.lynnhowardbooks.com

About the Author

Lynn Howard lives in Cedar Hill, MO, where all her sexy Shifters exist. She lives and breathes hot Alpha males and sassy, brassy females. She feels the most at home knee deep in mud and chicken muck and prefers to be outside under the stars, cuddled up under a blanket in front of a bonfire.

When not typing away or feeding her chickens, you can find her fantasizing about hot country boys for her next book or wandering the woods in search of wildlife. She loves all animals and insects…except spiders. Her favorite foot accessory is barefoot and she owns at least thirty sets of salt-n-pepper shakers, yet only uses one.

Gray's Wolf is the first in the Big River Pack series. And just like in Gray's Wolf, there are more hot country boy Shifters just waiting to their turn for a little love and romance.

Reading Order

Big River pack:
Gray's Wolf
Micah's Match
Emory's Mate
Reed's Girl
Tristan's Voice

Blackwater Clan:
Colton's Kitty
Noah's Fire
Carter's Devotion
Luke's Redemption

Ravenwood Pride:
Braxton's Warrior
Aron's Element
Daxon's Heart

Mason's Princess

Morse Pack:
Koda's Challenge
Auddi's Destiny
Zeke's Revelation

Shifter Council Executioners:
Shift in Priority
Shift in Focus
Shift in Supremacy